The

CARNIVAL

of

Wishes &

Dreams

ALSO BY JENNY LUNDQUIST

The CARNIVAL

of
Wishes &
Dreams

By Jenny Lundquist

Aladdin

New York London Toronto Sydney New Delhi

ALADDIN
An imprint of Simon & Schuster Children's Publishing Division
1230 Avenue of the Americas, New York, New York 10020
First Aladdin paperback edition February 2019
Text copyright © 2019 by Jenny Lundquist
Cover illustration copyright © 2019 by Erwin Madrid
Also available in an Aladdin hardcover edition.
All rights reserved, including the right of reproduction in whole or in part in any form.
ALADDIN and related logo are registered trademarks of Simon & Schuster, Inc.
For information about special discounts for bulk purchases,
please contact Simon & Schuster Special Sales at 1-866-506-1949
or business@simonandschuster.com.
The Simon & Schuster Speakers Bureau can bring authors to your live event. For more information or to book an event contact the Simon & Schuster Speakers Bureau at 1-866-248-3049 or visit our website at www.simonspeakers.com.
Book designed by Tiara Iandiorio
The text of this book was set in Brandon Grotesque.
Manufactured in the United States of America 0119 OFF
2 4 6 8 10 9 7 5 3 1
The Library of Congress has cataloged the hardcover edition as follows:
Names: Lundquist, Jenny, author.
Title: The Carnival of Wishes and Dreams / by Jenny Lundquist.
Description: First Aladdin hardcover edition. | New York : Aladdin, 2019. |
Summary: Told from three viewpoints, Audrey, Grace, and Harlow come together at their annual town carnival to heal and reconnect after a tragedy.
Identifiers: LCCN 2018015961 (print) | LCCN 2018025350 (eBook) |
ISBN 9781534416932 (eBook) | ISBN 9781534416918 (pbk) |
ISBN 9781534416925 (hc)
Subjects: | CYAC: Carnivals—Fiction. | Best friends—Fiction. |
Friendship—Fiction. | Emotional problems—Fiction.
Classification: LCC PZ7.L97886 (eBook) | LCC PZ7.L97886 Car 2019 (print) |
DDC [Fic]—dc23
LC record available at https://lccn.loc.gov/2018015961

TO LISA ALLEN:
You are an amazing person
and an inspiration to me.
I'm so glad we're sisters.

The
CARNIVAL
of
Wishes &
Dreams

▸ 1 ◂

Audrey

10 HOURS TO MIDNIGHT

COME TO THE CARNIVAL OF WISHES AND *Dreams. Meet me at the Ferris wheel at midnight. We'll ride it together.*

Audrey McKinley stared at the message on the pumpkin gram she'd just received and blinked. She didn't need an invitation; *of course* she was going to the carnival tonight. Everyone in Clarkville was going. It was the biggest social event of the entire year.

She twisted a strand of curly red hair around her finger and examined the rest of the note. Her name was written in big block letters in the space next to the "To" section. But the space next to the "From" section was blank. Had the sender just forgotten to sign their name? Or was the note intended to be anonymous?

Pumpkin grams were a big fall tradition at Clarkville Middle School. Students paid a dollar to write a special note to their friends on orange construction paper pumpkins, which were delivered at the end of the school day, a few hours before the carnival opened. The whole *point* was to know who sent them. To know who your friends were and just how many you had.

Seriously, why even bother sending one if you weren't going to sign it?

Audrey glanced up and looked around Miss Prescott's seventh-period math class. In the seat in front of her, Grace Chang was staring off into space. She considered asking Grace what she thought about the pumpkin gram, but since Audrey and Grace weren't supposed to talk to each other anymore, she decided against it. The members of the student government were still making deliveries, so she flagged down Lucas

Carter, who had dropped the pumpkin gram on her desk.

"Do you know who sent this?" she asked. "It's unsigned."

Lucas shook his head. "Maybe you have a secret admirer."

An anonymous note. A secret admirer. These were mysterious, wonderful things. But the message itself was not wonderful.

Audrey loved the Carnival of Wishes and Dreams—the fall festival that blew into town for one magical night every October. She loved the gold-and-crimson-striped tents; the carousel that some people swore could grant wishes; the way the carnival lights frosted everything with a golden glow; the way the whole evening smelled like popcorn and roasted peanuts. This year she especially loved that her dad had gotten a job operating one of the rides. It was good money, and she hoped they'd be able to make rent this month instead of falling behind again.

The only thing she *didn't* love was the Ferris wheel.

She was afraid of heights—everyone in town knew that. Last year when she'd tried to ride it she'd had a huge panic attack. She'd been sitting with Harlow Carlson— back when they were all still friends with Harlow—and Harlow had tried to keep her calm until their cart reached the bottom. After that, Audrey swore she'd never ride it again.

She made a quick list of everyone who had already sent her a pumpkin gram. It was a respectable haul, but still, none of that respectable haul included a pumpkin gram from Julia King, her best friend. Julia had been acting a little weird lately—maybe the message was her idea of a joke? Audrey pulled out her phone and texted Julia, who was sitting three seats up in the front row.

That's NOT funny.

Julia texted back: What's not funny?

The message you sent, Audrey answered.

Julia twisted around in her seat and mouthed, *What?*

In response, Audrey held up her pumpkin gram and frowned.

Julia pretended to smack her forehead, and a few

seconds later, she sent another text: Totally forgot to send you one.

Julia *forgot* to send her a pumpkin gram? Audrey knew for a *fact* that Julia had sent twenty pumpkin grams. So how could she forget to send one to her own best friend?

Audrey could only send five this year. She'd had to spend most of the birthday money Aunt Lisa gave her on groceries—and even then she'd felt bad about keeping five dollars for herself. It could have meant a couple extra boxes of cereal in their bare pantry, but instead she'd used it for pumpkin grams.

She looked down at the message. If it wasn't from Julia then it had to be from someone else. Someone who wanted to meet her at the Ferris wheel at midnight tonight.

But who?

▶ 2 ◀

Grace

GRACE CHANG HAD DONE A VERY BAD
thing.

Well, actually, she'd done several very bad things,
and the worst part of it was she couldn't tell anyone.
While everyone else in Miss Prescott's seventh-period
math class was opening pumpkin grams, Grace was staring straight ahead, feeling sick to her stomach.

The first very bad thing Grace had done was to tell
her mother the truth last night when she'd asked Grace
what she thought of her new hair color. Well, *colors,*

plural, because there were three of them. Her mother's once-long black hair was now a blue that faded to purple, then faded to pink, like a waterfall of color. Her mother said it was something called ombré.

"Your head looks like the top of an ice-cream cone," Grace had answered, and they both knew it was an insult. Grace didn't like ice cream; she was allergic to dairy.

Her mother's hair didn't really look like an ice-cream cone—or any other type of dessert—but actually cool and stylish, because she was a hairdresser. In Grace's opinion, mothers weren't supposed to look cool and stylish. But adults seldom want the truth when they ask for your opinion—they just want you to agree with them—so Grace knew it was her own fault when her mother got mad and grounded her.

Well, she didn't ground her just because of *that*. Her mother also grounded her because she'd received a note from school regarding Grace's lack of participation in class. It was the second very bad thing Grace had done. But in Grace's opinion there had been no lack; she'd simply been performing a scientific experiment: Exactly how long would it take her mother to figure out she wasn't bothering to do any classwork whatsoever?

Two and a half weeks, as it turned out, thanks to the note.

Her mother had flipped out and said she was sick of Grace's snarky attitude and that she'd better shape up, pronto, and start being nicer. But Grace didn't feel like being nice these days. Or happy. *You* try being happy when your mother up and announces you're moving in three weeks. One minute you're eating dinner and then . . . *BAM!* Just like that, no warning. Those three weeks were up tomorrow morning, when they'd climb into the huge moving truck her mother had rented and head to their new home in California, where her mother said the sun always shone.

Grace hated California. And sunshine.

Her mother said she needed to leave Clarkville because she couldn't handle the memories. Well, maybe *she* wanted to forget, but Grace did not. Sometimes

Grace wondered if leaving Clarkville meant she'd be leaving her dad's memory behind.

So now Grace was grounded, which was a very serious problem. She couldn't spend her last night in Clarkville stuck at home. She had overheard something she wasn't supposed to hear. Something that had to do with Harlow Carlson, the carnival, and—

A boy dropped a pumpkin gram on her desk and said, "Hi, Grace! Are you going to the carnival tonight?"

Grace tugged her lucky Cubs baseball cap down lower so no one would see the stupid grin spreading across her face. It wasn't just any boy standing in front of her; it was Diego Martinez, the student body president of the eighth grade and the boy she'd loved since forever. Or since the third grade, when he'd told off Ethan McKinley—Audrey McKinley's twin brother—after Ethan smacked her in the face with a dodgeball. Diego had hollered that you weren't supposed to hit girls, then he'd hauled off and socked Ethan in the stomach. He'd been Grace's hero ever since.

But Diego had definitely *not* been in love with Grace since the third grade. Probably because she rarely spoke to him, even though their families had been friends for years. She glanced down at her pumpkin gram and read the message:

Come to the Carnival of Wishes and Dreams. Meet me at the Ferris wheel at midnight. We'll ride it together.

A text came in from Julia King: Can't wait for tonight! I'm going out to dinner before the carnival with my parents. Want to come with us?

Grace's stomach was really heaving now. Because Julia had asked her to do something yesterday. Something important. And Grace hadn't done it. But Julia thought she had.

"Earth to Grace? Hello, anybody home?" A sweaty palm waved in front of her face. That palm belonged to Diego, who had been standing in front of her this whole time, waiting for Grace to answer his question.

"Sorry, what?" Grace said, looking up.

"I said, 'Are you going to the carnival tonight?'"

Having Diego stand so close to her was making it

hard to breathe, so she could only squeak out, "Why?"

"Well . . ." Diego looked like he really wanted to say something, and Grace's heart sped up and thundered in her ears. But the members of the student government were leaving now, so he just shook his head and said, "Never mind. Hope to see you there tonight."

He left and Grace let out a breath. That was the longest conversation they'd had in a while. And he hoped to see her tonight—her last night in Clarkville!

Except she was still grounded; she wasn't supposed to go to the carnival. And Grace always did what she was supposed to do.

She was like her dad in that way. He always did what he was supposed to do. Take running into burning buildings, for instance. That was his job, so he did it all the time. Except for that one time last year. He'd run into a burning building—a factory, actually—but he hadn't run back out. That was a whole other story, though, and Grace really didn't want to think about it right now.

But since she *was* thinking about it, it gave her another thought, one that has occurred to her a lot lately: Doing what you're supposed to do doesn't always work out that great. Maybe sometimes doing what you're *not* supposed to do is the way to go.

Miss Prescott had moved to the front of the class and was yammering on about fractions, but no one was paying any attention. Everyone was too excited about the pumpkin grams and the carnival. Grace didn't even know why the teachers made them go to school on the day of the carnival. It should be a holiday, in her opinion.

Grace had a lot of opinions, actually.

But even though she had lots of opinions in her head, she oftentimes had trouble turning them into words in her mouth. She was the quietest girl in the eighth grade. A lot of her classmates probably thought she was mute. Or maybe just a major dork. Of course, no one could ever actually *say* that. Not when she was friends with Julia King.

Which was why Grace definitely should have done the thing Julia asked her to do.

I can't go tonight, Grace finally texted Julia back. I'm grounded, remember?

Julia replied immediately: Can't you talk your mother into letting you off, just for tonight?

Grace gulped; she would be in so much trouble if Julia found out what Grace had not done. Maybe it was better that she was grounded and couldn't go tonight. Except for that thing that she'd overheard in the library the other day. If her ears could be trusted, then she absolutely *needed* to be at the carnival tonight.

Jeremy Johnson, the boy who sat next to her and never minded his own business, leaned over. "That's a strange message," he said, tapping her pumpkin gram. "Who sent it to you?"

Grace looked down. The space next to the word "From" was blank.

"No one," she answered.

▶ 3 ◀

Harlow

HARLOW CARLSON SAT AT THE BACK OF Miss Prescott's seventh-period math class, ignoring everyone, especially the members of the student government as they passed out pumpkin grams. Pumpkin grams at Clarkville Middle School were just one more way for the students to remind one another who was popular and well-liked, or, as was the case for Harlow, who was not.

Instead she was flipping through the pictures she'd snapped with her phone last weekend. They all featured important places in Clarkville: city hall, the abandoned textile mill, the old-fashioned lampposts on Main Street, the Clarkville Bridge. Her favorite shot by far was of the old water tower, the side of which bore the town's unofficial slogan in neat red paint:

CLARKVILLE
THE PLACE WHERE THE
PEOPLE YOU LOVE LIVE

Mrs. Murphy—the adviser for the yearbook club—had asked Harlow to take the photos so they could devote a couple pages to the town itself this year. It was extra work on top of her normal duties as the editor of the yearbook, but Harlow didn't mind. After all, she didn't have much else to do on the weekends.

She kept scrolling and realized she'd forgotten to take a picture of the town wishing well. She glanced outside the window. The sunlight was deep and golden; a perfect autumn afternoon. She'd ask her mom if they could make a small detour on the way home today so she could get the shot.

Lucas Carter passed by and plopped an orange

construction paper pumpkin on her desk. Harlow figured it must be a mistake. But when she tried to hand it back to him he wouldn't take it.

"It has your name on it," he said. "Look."

Harlow looked; he was right, it *did* have her name on it. The sender hadn't bothered to sign it and he—or she—had written an odd message:

Come to the Carnival of Wishes and Dreams. Meet me at the Ferris wheel at midnight. We'll ride it together.

Harlow still thought it might be a mistake. No one at school wanted to meet her at the carnival, just like no one wanted to sit next to her in class or in the cafeteria.

Last year she wouldn't have thought it was a mistake. She would have *expected* to receive a pumpkin gram. A whole pile of them, actually; more than anyone else, even Julia King. But that was before the fire.

Even if it was a mistake, Harlow took her phone out of her backpack and snapped a picture of the pumpkin gram. This was a moment; she wanted to capture it. Harlow collected moments the way some people collected coins, or maybe marbles. She took another shot, this time zooming in just to catch the first line: *Come to the Carnival of Wishes and Dreams* . . .

After she put her phone away, she glanced out the window again. Beyond the football field the wheat fields stretched to the horizon. A few miles away, at the end of Hilltop Street, the carnival would already be set up; a shadow against the cornflower sky, waiting for the sun to set, for the clock to strike six, when the wrought iron gates would be unlocked and the residents of Clarkville would go charging inside.

She looked at the message again: *Meet me at the Ferris wheel at midnight.*

A cloud inched across the sky, a shadow crept into the classroom, and a chill raced down Harlow's spine.

Then again, maybe the note *wasn't* a mistake. Lots of things weren't mistakes. Like when she went to sit at Julia's cafeteria table last week. She thought maybe enough time had passed and things would be okay again. She'd thought wrong. So maybe it was a joke, a really nasty one. Maybe whoever sent the note was just waiting for her to show up at the Ferris wheel at midnight, only for there to be no one waiting.

Or—she thought back to the dead sardine someone had shoved in her locker yesterday—maybe someone *would* be waiting for Harlow. Someone who thought it would be funny to play another prank on her.

Harlow stared out the window and absently scratched at her nose, trying to puzzle it out. Who wanted to meet her at midnight, and why? She hadn't even been planning on going to the carnival tonight. Mostly because she didn't have anyone to go with.

Except earlier today Mrs. Murphy said she expected Harlow to take tons of pictures of the carnival. So in a way, it was sort of her *job* to go.

Harlow loved taking pictures. She just wished every once in a while someone would want to be in a picture *with* her, but lately the only time anyone even smiled at her was when she was staring at them through the lens of her camera phone. Otherwise, ever since the fire, everyone pretended like she didn't exist.

Like right now, for instance. Harlow glanced down and saw a spider crawling toward Erin Donoghue's open backpack. Harlow bit back a scream and forced herself to take deep breaths, feeling foolish. It was just a small spider, after all. She didn't know why they scared her so much. "Erin," she whispered urgently. "Erin!"

Erin was sitting right next to her; there's no way she didn't hear Harlow's call. But Erin didn't acknowledge her at all. She didn't turn her head; she didn't even blink.

"Erin, there's a spider—" Harlow began, but it didn't matter. Lucas Carter came by again to drop a pumpkin gram on Erin's desk, and squashed the spider with his sneaker. Erin ignored Harlow and thanked Lucas.

A pang echoed through Harlow's middle. For the last year, she had felt a huge sense of loss. Like waking up one day and finding out something that should be there suddenly isn't. Kind of like those people who lose an arm or a leg but their phantom limb itches anyway.

Harlow had a phantom limb. Well, limbs, plural—one for every friend she lost last year. The itching was at its worst when everyone talked and left her out. Because even though Miss Prescott had stopped speaking and the class was quiet now, everyone was talking. Texting, actually. Whole conversations were happening as students tapped on cell phones hidden in their laps. Plans were being made and jokes were being told, but it was all being done silently. The only noise in the room at all was the humming of the air conditioner and the sound of a pencil rolling off a desk.

And the soft clicking of a camera shutter.

Harlow snapped out of her thoughts and looked over, but all she saw was Erin tapping innocently on her phone. On the other side of Erin sat Ethan McKinley, scowling because Miss Prescott had given him detention for hiding all the erasable markers again. Still, she felt something like dread ballooning in her heart.

That settled it. Yearbook or not, she was definitely not going tonight.

▶ 4 ◀

Audrey

9 HOURS TO MIDNIGHT

THE LAST FIVE MINUTES ON THE BUS WERE the hardest for Audrey. Each day her stomach twisted itself into knots as she waited for the McKinley residence to come into view. Many times she wished Mrs. Pearson, the bus driver, would pass her house altogether and keep going. She oftentimes liked to imagine herself riding off to another town. To another life.

But then she'd think of Maddie and Mason, her two younger siblings, and wonder who would cook them dinner if she left—Ethan couldn't be counted on, since lately he was spending his entire life in detention—and she knew she had to get off the bus.

Next to her, Julia was tapping away on her cell, and Audrey's own phone buzzed with a text. It was from Julia.

To: Audrey, Erin, Lulu, Grace

Bad news, guys! My parents said I could only invite two people to my birthday party. They are SO mean!

Audrey's heart sank. Julia had been talking forever about the epic birthday party her parents were letting her plan: A limo drive into the city for dinner at a fancy restaurant and then a play afterward. They had all been really looking forward to it. Now only two of them could go with Julia? How would she choose who to take?

Audrey, Grace, and Harlow had become friends with Julia, Lulu, and Erin when the six of them all ended up in Mrs. Bronson's class in fourth grade. Back then, their friendship was sealed by everyone's love for lip gloss and Harry Potter. They still ate lunch together, but things were a lot more complicated now. Julia was their unofficial leader and by far the most popular girl in their group—especially since no one could stand Harlow anymore.

Both Julia and Audrey's phones began buzzing with texts from the other girls:

Erin: I want to go!

Lulu: I love going to the city!

Audrey loved going to the city too. Should she text that to Julia and say so? They were sitting *right next* to each other. Maybe she should say something in person? But she had a feeling Julia wouldn't like that. Julia was already in a bad mood since she'd gotten stuck watching Simon, her science class's guinea pig, this weekend. His cage was wedged in the bus walkway because Julia refused to set it on her lap.

Julia once told Audrey that if you couldn't capture a moment on your phone, it might as well have never happened at all—wise advice that Audrey remembered now.

"Want to take a selfie?" Audrey asked.

Julia looked up immediately. "Sure," she answered.

After they were both done straightening their hair,

they smiled widely as Audrey pointed her phone at them. "Say 'Birthday girl!'"

"Birthday girl!" they shouted.

Audrey posted the photo online with the caption Hanging with my BFF.

There. A little reminder never hurt.

"Look," said Julia. "There's Harlow."

Audrey glanced out the window. Just before her breath fogged up the glass, she spied Mrs. Carlson's fancy SUV charging by, kicking up a crust of dust. She could just make out Harlow's dark hair in the passenger seat as the SUV sped up and pulled in front of the old lumbering school bus, then turned off the road in the direction of the town's old wishing well.

"I'll bet Harlow's never ridden a bus a day in her life," Julia added, her lip curled in disgust.

Audrey knew that, actually, Harlow had ridden on a bus exactly once, but since she never liked discussing Harlow she changed the subject. "Are you going to the carnival tonight?" she asked.

"Duh," Julia said as if the answer were obvious.

But it wasn't obvious to Audrey, not exactly. Sure, everyone was going to the carnival, but every time Audrey had tried to make plans this week, Julia avoided giving her a direct answer.

"You could come over to my house," Audrey said. "We could walk to the carnival together."

"Can't," Julia answered. "Our family is going to Frank's Diner tonight for dinner."

"There's still time before dinner," Audrey said. "Want to come over for a while?"

"No thanks."

"Why not?" Audrey asked, although she had a sinking feeling she already knew.

"My parents don't want me hanging out at your house anymore." Julia fixed her with an imperious stare and Audrey wondered if she needed to apologize for something. Julia often had that effect on people.

But since she wasn't exactly sure what she should be apologizing *for*, she said, "Oh, sure."

"Look, it's not a big deal, okay?" Julia said, sounding impatient. "Why don't you just meet us for dinner?"

Audrey was tempted to stall, to not let Julia see how much the invitation meant to her, but she didn't want Julia to get any more irritated. "Okay, thanks," she said, just as the bus lurched up to her house.

"Great," Julia said. "And hey—could you do me a favor? Could you watch Simon for me? I'm really busy this weekend."

"Sure, I'd love to!" Audrey lied in a cheerful voice. The truth was she couldn't stand guinea pigs or their smelly cages. But she didn't want to tell Julia no—not right after she'd invited Audrey to dinner. And, hey, maybe Julia would remember this when she decided which friends to take to her birthday party.

Audrey picked up Simon's cage, wrinkling her nose at the smell. She turned to wave to Julia just as the doors hissed shut behind her.

The McKinleys lived in a rickety two-story rental where broken things didn't get fixed. The front lawn was brown and littered with bits of trash. Audrey dragged herself up the steps of the porch, careful to skip the second one, which was wobbly. Normally in the fall the

McKinleys' porch was decorated with pimply pumpkins and multicolored squashes. But this year, with Mrs. McKinley gone, no one had remembered to buy them.

Audrey wondered where her mother was right this very minute. Was she nearby? Did she remember that tonight was the Carnival of Wishes and Dreams?

Audrey paused at the front door; she couldn't stand their rental house. They'd had to leave their home on Hudson Road—the one her parents bought right after they got married—one gray morning last spring while the neighbors watched and whispered "foreclosure" behind cupped hands like it was a dirty word, the kind that tastes like soap in your mouth. Except Audrey was pretty sure no one in their family had done anything wrong. Her mother didn't seem to share that opinion; as far as Audrey could tell, she seemed to think it was her father's fault for not being able to find another job after the factory burned down. Audrey hadn't thought that was fair. A lot of men hadn't been able to find work after they lost their jobs at the factory.

She blew out a breath, squared her shoulders,

and opened the front door. Maddie and Mason were sprawled out on the couch, watching a movie. The bluish glare from the television flickered across two identical heads, four eyes, and twenty fingers. Mason and Maddie were twins. So were Audrey and Ethan. Audrey's mom and Aunt Lisa were twins, too; it ran in their family. It was just a myth that twins skipped a generation, but everyone always stared when the McKinleys went out in town together. They all had the same curly red hair, the same clear green eyes, and skin so pale that Julia once told Audrey they all looked like a bunch of bloodsucking vampires.

The McKinley Family Freak Show, Ethan called them. *Where you can get two for the price of one.*

"No TV before homework," Audrey said after she'd deposited Simon's cage in the kitchen.

"It's Friday," Maddie answered, stretching her feet out on the coffee table. Empty soda cans and crumpled chip bags covered the rest of the table. They'd stay there until Audrey picked them up.

"But if you do it now," Audrey reasoned, "then you'll

have the whole rest of the weekend free." It sounded like something an adult would say; Audrey was proud of herself for thinking of it.

In answer, Maddie rolled her eyes and Mason turned up the volume on the TV.

Audrey wanted to send them to their rooms for being rude, but she wasn't sure she could get away with it. After all, she was their sister, not their mother.

"Where's Dad?" she asked.

"He's sleeping," Mason answered, not taking his eyes off the TV.

"I'm hungry," Maddie said, also not looking away from the screen. "Are you making dinner tonight?"

In the last two months, "dinner" at the McKinleys had consisted of scrambled eggs, quesadillas, or spaghetti—the only things Audrey knew how to cook. Last week she'd attempted roast chicken, canned green beans, and mashed potatoes from a box. It hadn't worked out too well.

Tonight she didn't have to cook because Maddie and Mason were sleeping over at Aunt Lisa and Uncle Dan's house so Audrey could have a night to herself and go to the carnival with her friends.

After telling Maddie and Mason to pack their things because Uncle Dan would be here soon, Audrey went to her room and spent the next twenty minutes trying to decide what to wear to the carnival. There would be so many pictures posted online tonight; she needed to look her best.

Audrey worked extremely hard at cultivating her online image. She frequently practiced her camera-ready smile. She posted selfies all the time. Every time she went somewhere with her friends, she was always looking for an opportunity to post another photo. Last night she'd posted a video of herself twirling her baton while she simultaneously ate an ice-cream cone. She'd gotten a ton of likes, but no new followers, which was disappointing.

Audrey and Julia had been competing to see who could get to three hundred online followers first. Right now they were tied, with just two more to go. Audrey was determined to win and get those two extra followers tonight.

Online, Audrey was just as popular as Julia—something Audrey was secretly really proud of.

Popularity wasn't the only reason she was working so hard to create a shiny Internet life. She had been doing everything she could possibly think of to earn extra money. Babysitting her cousins. Recycling cans. Last month, she started her own YouTube channel so she could make money from ads—it was a DIY channel where Audrey could show people how to make crafts—except it was going to take her way too long to get enough subscribers. Also, it turned out she was awful at crafts.

But just last week she found the opportunity of a lifetime: A new web series about middle-school kids called *Middle School Daze* was accepting online auditions, and Audrey was determined to put together a killer submission package. She thought she had a great shot—she was the star of the school play last year and had done an amazing job. Everyone said so.

She texted Julia: I'm thinking of wearing my turquoise sweater tonight.

Both Audrey and Julia owned the exact same

turquoise sweater. They bought them together when they went back-to-school shopping over the summer. They were supposed to text each other to make sure they didn't wear them on the same day. Or at least Audrey was supposed to text Julia.

Julia texted back right away: I'm wearing that tonight.

Okay, Audrey texted. I'll wear something else.

Audrey smiled; she hadn't actually been planning on wearing the turquoise sweater. But now she had a written record. When she showed up tonight in her sparkly black sweater—another item they both owned—Julia couldn't get mad. Audrey figured sometimes friends could be a little difficult, but that was okay. You just had to learn to work with them.

Speaking of being difficult: A lot of people would be wearing costumes to the carnival tonight, and Julia had decided they'd all wear tiaras and red feather boas as their costume, mainly because Mrs. King had a really nice crystal tiara she said Julia could wear. Audrey wasn't so lucky, so after she finished picking out the rest of her outfit—a pair of jeans, black boots, and dangly earrings—

she threw on the feather boa she'd gotten at the dollar store and the tiara she'd made out of glittery pipe cleaners. Then she set up her phone on her dresser and pushed the record button.

"Hi!" she said to the camera. "My name is Audrey McKinley. I'm in eighth grade, and I am your next star of *Middle School Daze*! I live in—"

She paused. Was she coming across as too cocky? Was it dumb to film her audition introduction while she was wearing her costume? And how did her hair look anyway?

She checked her phone, only to discover the video had frozen even before she'd started speaking. Her phone was several years old—it was her mother's old castoff—and didn't work well anymore.

"Stupid piece of junk," she muttered. She'd have to try recording later. She shoved her phone into her pocket, then headed for her parents' room.

In her mind, it was still her parents' room, not just her dad's room, because she was positive that any day now her mother would come back. She would be able to sense how much Audrey needed her. She would feel it the way you could feel the wind ruffling the wheat fields that surrounded Clarkville.

Mrs. McKinley had taken off two months ago on a sweltering morning in August, claiming that she just couldn't *do* it anymore. Audrey didn't blame her for leaving—she knew her mother wasn't always herself when she stopped taking her medication—but many days she wished she could have gone with her to wher-ever she was now.

Deep snores issued from behind the closed door, and for just a moment, Audrey allowed herself to imag-ine driving away in the old school bus to that shiny new life. A life where moms didn't leave just because things had gotten difficult. Where dads didn't stay out all night with their friends. A life where magical things could still happen. She pulled the unsigned pumpkin gram from her pocket and stared at the message.

Come to the Carnival of Wishes and Dreams. Meet me at the Ferris wheel at midnight. We'll ride it together.

The note seemed magical, and more than a little

mysterious. Who would ask her to ride the Ferris wheel when practically everyone in town knew she was afraid of heights?

She stuffed the note back into her pocket and knocked on the door. When she opened it, her father was just emerging from under a pile of blankets, red-eyed and unshaven. The scars on his right arm seemed even redder today. Audrey averted her eyes so he wouldn't catch her staring. He'd gotten them last year on the night of the fire, when Henry Chang pulled him out of the factory.

"It's nearly four," she said. "What time do you have to be at the carnival?"

"Food," Mr. McKinley mumbled.

"But—"

"Now," he said.

A little while later in the kitchen, while he was forking a bite of the scrambled eggs Audrey had made him, she asked, "What ride are you operating tonight?"

"The Ferris wheel," he answered.

5

Grace

7 HOURS TO MIDNIGHT

GRACE HAD BEEN GROUNDED BEFORE. Plenty of times, in fact.

Like the time she, Audrey, and Harlow had tried to run away from home. Or the time she'd sneaked Audrey into her house in the middle of the night because Audrey was sick of hearing her parents scream at each other. Audrey had run away across their neighborhood to Grace's house, and the two of them stayed up all night listening to music and chatting online with Harlow.

Or the time Grace had socked Ethan in the stomach and knocked the wind out of him. It was only a couple weeks after her father died and it was her first day back at school. She'd come upon Ethan in the halls, laughing with his friends. *Laughing.* Like everything was normal. Like the entire world hadn't just ended. It had made Grace so mad, but like usual she couldn't find the right words. Instead she'd found her right fist.

But this time was totally different since tonight was Grace's last night in Clarkville. A fact her mother seemed determined to ignore.

"What about this one?" Mrs. Chang held up yet another dress in front of the mirror, this one a blue-and-yellow floral print. For someone moving tomorrow, her mother didn't seem concerned that half the contents of her closet were spread out all over her bed.

"It clashes with your hair," Grace said.

Grace was helping her mother pick out an outfit to wear to her book club meeting tonight. She was also simultaneously checking her phone for new developments. Ever since Julia texted that only two people could go to her birthday party and Audrey had posted that BFF picture, Lulu had been texting Grace and Erin all afternoon trying to figure out *what it all meant*. Things had only gotten worse now that Audrey had started posting pictures online of her dinner with the Kings.

Why didn't they invite us? Another text from Lulu arrived. I love Frank's Diner!

I don't know. I love Frank's too! Erin texted.

Grace didn't text much, just like she didn't talk much, so no one had directly asked her if she'd been invited to the dinner. She decided to pretend she hadn't.

"Grace," Mrs. Chang said, sounding irritated. "Put your phone down and help me." She held up a pink and gray dress. "What about this one?"

"Getting closer," Grace said. "I don't know why you're going out tonight—shouldn't we finish packing?"

"Everything's nearly done." Mrs. Chang spread her arms wide, taking in the bare room. "Besides, it's my last night to get together with the book club," she added, and Grace sighed.

While her mother would be out with her friends

enjoying her last night in Clarkville, Grace would be stuck at home, alone. It wasn't fair.

"What about this one?" Mrs. Chang plucked another dress from the pile. A long-sleeved floral one.

"It's ugly and it makes you look eighty years old."

Mrs. Chang frowned. "Can you at least *try* to have a good attitude? When we get to California you might actually like it. We'll be in driving distance to both the Angels and Dodgers' stadiums. You'll have your pick of baseball teams."

As far as Grace was concerned, both the Dodgers and the Angels could kiss her big toe. She was a Cubs fan, just like her dad had been. If he were still alive he'd have been shocked at even the thought of rooting for another team. Of course, if her dad was still alive they wouldn't have been moving in the first place.

"We're in this together, you know," Mrs. Chang added. "We're a team. Team Chang, remember?"

Grace swallowed. "I remember," she said quietly.

The truth was, even if she was mad, Grace would do anything for her mother. That's why when her mother said she didn't want them to associate with the McKinley and Carlson families anymore, Grace had stopped speaking to Harlow and Audrey—which was the hardest thing Grace ever had to do, especially since she and Audrey still sat at the same lunch table. But she'd wanted to make her mother happy, so she'd done it anyway. They were Team Chang—the only two people left on the team now, and they needed to stick together.

But staying home, grounded, on her last night in Clarkville? Missing the Carnival of Wishes and Dreams? It was too much.

"When are you coming home?" Grace asked.

"Probably not until pretty late, I think."

"What am I supposed to eat for dinner?"

Their refrigerator, along with the contents of their pantry, was packed up in the moving truck that was parked outside their house. Grace secretly hoped someone would steal it overnight.

"There's money on the kitchen counter if you want to order pizza. Or there's a pack of microwaveable pasta—just add hot water from the sink and it should be fine."

In Grace's opinion, microwaveable pasta was disgusting. So was pizza, since she always had to order it dairy free.

"Can I go to the carnival tonight?" Grace asked. "I want to eat a funnel cake."

"You're grounded, remember?" Mrs. Chang frowned and held up another dress. "What about this one?"

"Why do you even care what you wear tonight? It's just your stupid book club," Grace grumbled. "Can't you make an exception just this once? I can be grounded an extra night in California. I really want to go to the carnival—everyone in school is going. It's not fair."

"*Life* isn't fair," Mrs. Chang said. "Get used to it."

They were both quiet then, because more than most people, Grace and her mother knew just how *not fair* life could be.

Grace hadn't wanted to do this, but she'd been left with no other choice. For multiple reasons she needed to be at the carnival tonight. She pulled her pumpkin gram from her pocket and placed it on top of the dress pile.

"Someone sent you this?" Mrs. Chang asked after picking it up and reading it.

"A boy dropped it on my desk this afternoon when they passed them all out," Grace answered. She didn't add that boy had been Diego Martinez or that she wished *he* had sent it. She knew he hadn't; that would constitute a grand gesture, and she was pretty sure Diego wasn't capable of something like that. In fact, the only gesture most of the boys in her class were capable of making was an obscene one involving their middle finger.

Mrs. Chang frowned. "It's unsigned—do you know who wrote it?" When Grace didn't respond, she added, "Were any of your classmates behaving strangely around you?"

"Not any stranger than usual," Grace said.

"I know you think I'm too strict, but I don't like the idea of you going out at night to meet some mystery person. Anyone could have written this note. It could be from an ax murderer, or a kidnapper, or an escaped convict."

Grace was disappointed. She'd thought her mother would think the note was so exciting she'd let her have the night off from being grounded. But really, she should have known better.

"An escaped convict didn't write it," Grace said.

"This is a pumpkin gram. From *school*. The only people who were allowed to send them were students, or teachers, or maybe parents. You always—"

"You don't know *who* wrote it," Mrs. Chang interrupted. "You don't know *why* they want to meet you. Or *what* they plan to do when you get there." Her mother was working herself into one of her frenzies now, and Grace knew she needed to put a stop to it; otherwise she might not get to leave the house, ever.

"It'll be *fine*, Mom. The carnival isn't going to catch fire." The words pelted from Grace's mouth like poisonous arrows, and as they struck her mother, Grace wished she could pull them back, one by one.

She remembered the haunted look in her mother's eyes in the days immediately following the fire, and how she kept looking at the front door, expecting Grace's dad to walk through any minute.

Now her mother never expected the front door to open; it seemed she preferred it stayed shut, at least as far as Grace was concerned. She didn't just worry about fires anymore; she worried about illnesses and earthquakes and robbers and thieves and now, apparently, bad people who wrote anonymous pumpkin grams and were plotting to kidnap nice kids like Grace.

If her mother had her way, Grace would never leave the house, ever. If you stayed inside, you could never get hurt. You would be safe. Her mother, who used to be so laid back, hardly let Grace do anything anymore. In fact, Grace had a sneaking suspicion her mother was secretly glad she was grounded. It gave her an excuse to tell Grace she couldn't go out tonight.

But her mother wasn't following her own rules. She was dyeing her hair like a teenager and going out with her book club.

Grace was tired of being stuck inside the house. Stuck inside her own head. She wanted her last night in Clarkville to be unforgettable. Besides all of the other reasons she needed to be at the carnival, she wanted to eat a funnel cake and to see Diego one last time, even if she never actually spoke to him. She wanted to take a ride on the carousel—the one that some people in town swore was magic—and make some wishes.

Tonight she was on Team Grace.

Later, just as her mother was getting ready to leave, she turned to Grace and said, "Be good tonight."

Grace crossed her fingers behind her back and answered, "I will."

Mrs. Chang held out her arms and said goodbye, but Grace quickly sidestepped her and opened the front door. Grace hated hugs. And goodbyes.

After her mother was gone, Grace went and took the money from the counter. She was going to use it, but not for pizza.

Just before she opened the door and stepped outside—draped in the stupid red feather boa and plastic tiara Julia was making them all wear—she left what she thought was a fitting, non-anonymous note for her mother:

> It's my last night in Clarkville.
> I'm going to the carnival.
> Where the lights are so bright.
> I'll see you early tomorrow, before the sky turns light.

6

Harlow

THE QUICKEST WAY TO KNOW HOW MUCH
fun you're missing is to check your classmates' social
media accounts.

Harlow spent a ton of time online looking at pictures of all the things they did without her. Tonight,
for example, Julia King and Audrey McKinley were at
Frank's Diner having a pre-carnival dinner. They were
both wearing tiaras and feather boas, although Julia's
getup was much nicer than Audrey's. Harlow kept
refreshing her phone screen, not wanting to miss any-

thing. If she concentrated hard enough, she could pretend she was at Frank's, too, instead of in her kitchen with her mother, putting together welcome packets.

"Are you *sure* you don't want to go to the carnival?" Mrs. Carlson said as she stapled another packet.

"I'm sure," Harlow said, still looking at her phone. Audrey had just posted a picture of her and Julia smiling in front of the biggest banana split Harlow had ever seen with the caption *Not sure we can finish this!* Harlow grimaced and put her phone away. Then she picked up her own stapler and got to work. The packets had to be finished before her mother left for the carnival.

"*Why* don't you want to go?" Mrs. Carlson persisted. "You love the carnival."

"Well, I don't love it anymore," Harlow answered.

"Why not?"

Harlow concentrated on her stapler and didn't answer. She couldn't tell her mother the truth: that she had absolutely no one to go with and no friends at all.

It hadn't always been that way. She used to imagine Clarkville Middle School as her own personal kingdom.

With a flick of her wrist, someone would bring her lunch or offer to carry her backpack. She felt like a queen. But she should have paid more attention in history class. If she had, she'd have known that sometimes queens are overthrown. All it takes is a spark of unrest. Or, in her case, a huge fire that changes everything.

"I just don't feel like it," Harlow said. She stood up from her stool in front of the kitchen island and nearly smacked her head on a copper pan dangling from a hook overhead.

Harlow had gone through a huge growth spurt over the summer, and as a result she was now extremely tall, like her mother. But where her mother seemed glamorous, like a model, Harlow was coltish and awkward, with knobby knees and achy legs and slow reflexes. She was struggling on the tennis team this year, something Julia never failed to point out during team practice. Harlow had told her mother maybe it was time she quit the tennis team. In response, her mother hired a private coach and doubled Harlow's practice schedule.

Because that's just what you did when you were a

Carlson: When things got tough, you worked harder. Things had gotten really tough for the Carlsons—for most of Clarkville, actually—since the fire, and both her parents were working like mad to make things better for everyone.

Tonight, some potential investors from Boston were coming into town. Harlow's dad was taking them out, first to dinner, then to the carnival. Then first thing tomorrow morning he was going to present a proposal to them, asking for funds to help him reopen the factory. Between her father's slick spreadsheets and her mother's easy charm, they hoped tonight was finally the night things would start to turn around.

Harlow picked up the packets and took them over to the long back counter, where she began stuffing them into embossed blue folders that read **WELCOME TO CLARKVILLE** on the front.

The Carlsons' kitchen was nearly the size of the McKinley's old house on Hudson Road. (Harlow knew this because she and Audrey once measured it.) It was the kind of kitchen with copper pots hanging from the ceiling that no one used except Alex, the Carlsons' personal chef, and had strange appliances no one except Alex used lining the countertops. The only time the Carlsons used the kitchen themselves was when Harlow and her mother stuffed welcome packets for the latest round of investors Harlow's father brought to town.

"I still think you should go to the carnival," Mrs. Carlson said, joining Harlow at the counter. "You never know what surprises you might find tonight."

Harlow stopped stuffing and turned to her mother. "What does *that* mean?" she asked.

"Nothing, darling. It's just that it's the Carnival of Wishes and Dreams. All sorts of amazing things could happen."

Mrs. Carlson began stuffing the packets into the folders, seemingly innocent. But a thought lodged itself in Harlow's brain like a splinter: What if *her mother* had sent the unsigned pumpkin gram? How embarrassing would *that* be? She obviously knew Harlow had no intention of attending the carnival—Harlow had been telling her parents so all week—so maybe sending her an anonymous pumpkin gram was just her way of persuading her to go?

An electronic ping sounded, and Mrs. Carlson checked her phone. "That was your dad," she told Harlow. "Their flight arrived on time but there's a ton of traffic getting out of the city. After they get to the carnival, he'll take them to the city council tent where the council members and I will be waiting to meet them."

Harlow nodded as she checked her own phone. Comments were already pouring in on Audrey's banana split picture:

Lulu Pepperton: I can help you eat it haha!

Erin Donoghue: You both look so pretty, can't wait to meet up!

Lulu Pepperton: Should I come to the diner? ☺

Harlow felt for Lulu; she wished *she* could join them at the diner too. She sighed and put her phone down. She didn't know why she stalked her classmates' accounts; it only made her feel worse afterward.

She went back to helping her mother. When they were finished, Mrs. Carlson stretched and said, "All right. I think that's it. The gift baskets are already loaded up in the car." She rubbed her neck. "I have a really good feeling. I think tonight's the night—I can feel it."

Harlow wished she could share her mother's hopefulness. The thing was, her father was great at pitching a proposal (and a baseball, for that matter), but all the spreadsheets and welcome baskets in the world couldn't tell a story. They couldn't show all the tiny, beautiful moments that make up a town. They couldn't explain that Clarkville was special. So far none of the investors her father had brought to town had been able to see that.

Harlow and her mother loaded up the car with the welcome packets and Mrs. Carlson said, "Last chance. Are you sure you don't want to come tonight?"

Harlow nodded. "I'm sure."

After her mother drove away, Harlow checked her phone again. Audrey had just posted another photo. Now she and Julia were sipping sodas with licorice whips for straws.

Harlow figured they must be having the best time ever.

7

Audrey

AUDREY WAS HAVING THE WORST TIME ever.

But you'd never know it; not from the selfies Online Audrey posted. Online Audrey smiled brightly every time the camera flashed her way. Online Audrey smiled when Julia had them pose in front of the diner's sign. She smiled when Julia decided she wanted to eat dessert before dinner and asked Audrey to snap a selfie with the huge banana split they ordered. She smiled like she was having the time of her life.

Real-Life Audrey wished she was having half as much fun as Online Audrey.

In real life Julia had frowned when she'd seen Audrey in her sparkly black sweater and said, "I wish you'd told me you were wearing that." Mrs. King had also frowned when she'd seen Audrey. Julia must have seen the look, too, because she said, "I invited Audrey earlier this afternoon. That's okay, right, Mom?" Mrs. King, who rarely said no to Julia, had smiled and said it was totally fine—but Audrey knew it totally wasn't.

Then, when their hamburgers and sodas arrived, Julia decided they should use some of the licorice whips she had as straws. There must have been a hole in Audrey's, because when she went to slurp her root beer it spurted out the side and all over her chin and neck. Of course, you couldn't see *that* in the picture they posted.

Now Audrey was wet and sticky, but Julia didn't seem to notice; she was too busy talking about her birthday party and how much fun it would be cruising into the city in a limo. Audrey was assuming one of the two invitations belonged to her—she *was* Julia's best friend, after all—but technically Julia hadn't actually invited her yet.

"So, Audrey," Mr. King said, "What's your dad been up to these days?"

She knew he was just making polite conversation, but she didn't know how to answer his question. The truth was she had no clue what her dad was up to. Sometimes Audrey would catch him on the phone late at night, talking softly so no one could hear. He slept all day and was out all night. When she'd asked him where he went, he'd said he was working, but when she'd asked where, he had just waved her off and told her not to worry about it.

"He's good," she answered finally. "He's working at the carnival tonight."

Mrs. King, who had left the diner to go purchase their tickets to the carnival, reappeared then. "Just in time," she said, sliding back into the booth. "There's a huge line." She passed the tickets around the table. When she came to Audrey she said, "That'll be ten dollars, please."

"What? Oh . . ." A flush spread across Audrey's cheeks, and she didn't know what to say. Her father had received a couple free tickets for working at the carnival, and he'd given them to Audrey and Ethan. When Mrs. King had said she was going to purchase tickets, she hadn't mentioned she was planning to buy one for Audrey, too.

Mr. King, seeing Audrey's look and mistaking it for something else, said, "Don't worry, Audrey. We'll get it."

Mrs. King opened her mouth to say something, but upon seeing the look Mr. King shot her, closed it and focused on her milkshake.

Audrey slipped the ticket into her pocket, right next to the other one she carried. She quietly resumed eating her hamburger. While Julia continued to talk, Audrey looked around the diner. Pictures of Clarkville High's baseball team were tacked to the walls. Hanging over the order-up counter was a picture of the team from more than twenty years ago. Standing in the middle of everyone was their star hitter, Grace's dad, Henry "Home Run" Chang. On either side of Mr. Chang were his two best friends: shortstop Jimmy McKinley, Audrey's dad, and pitcher Russ Carlson, Harlow's dad.

Back when they were in high school, Audrey's, Grace's, and Harlow's fathers had been inseparable. It didn't matter that Mr. Chang's parents had grown up in Taiwan, or that Mr. Carlson's parents owned the largest house in Clarkville, or that Mr. McKinley's parents lived in Sterling Meadows—the trailer park at the edge of town everyone pretended didn't exist. They had loved baseball and one another. Their three families had done everything together. Up until nearly a year ago, when the fire changed everything.

This year's high school baseball team had a big game coming up tomorrow night against their rival, Fairvale High. This would be the first year the McKinleys, Carlsons, and Changs wouldn't watch it together. Audrey couldn't help but wonder if Harlow or Grace had thought about that at all.

"Audrey—did you hear what I said?" Julia said, sounding annoyed. "Pass me the ketchup."

You forgot to say please, Audrey almost retorted.

After the ketchup was safely in Julia's outstretched hands, Audrey excused herself to go refill her soda.

"Can you do me a favor and refill mine too?" Julia said, holding up her cup.

"Sure," Audrey said. After the drinks were refilled, she lingered at the soda fountain, not quite ready to go back to the table. She pulled out the unsigned pumpkin gram and stared at it. She'd almost told Julia about it earlier, but at the last minute she'd changed her mind. It felt like her own private secret; something you couldn't text or post or Photoshop. Something a little bit magical. Because who was this mysterious sender who wanted to meet her?

Just then her phone buzzed with a text. It was from Ethan:

Do you know where Dad is?

No, why? Audrey texted back.

Waiting at the carnival gates. Someone said he hasn't shown up for his shift yet.

Audrey sighed as she tapped out her response: He was still at home when I left.

The next text Ethan sent contained a ton of bad words neither of them were supposed to say. A lump formed in Audrey's throat as she deleted it. As she was leaving earlier her father had assured her he was nearly ready to go. "Just need to put a little more gas in my tank," he'd said, raising his coffee cup in salute. Now she wished she hadn't been so eager to meet Julia for dinner. She should have stayed home and made sure he got to work on time.

He's probably just running late.

Just as she sent her text, she heard Mr. and Mrs. King's hushed voices. They were in front of the cash register, waiting to pay the bill. Audrey, standing behind a fake tree near the soda fountain, was hidden from view.

"We're always paying for that girl," Mrs. King was saying.

"Keep your voice down," Mr. King said.

"I will not—Why can't the McKinleys pay for their own kind? That's what I want to know."

"They've had a tough run of luck, Doris," Mr. King retorted. "You *know* that."

"We've *all* had a tough run of luck—what excuse is that? You lost your job just the same as Jimmy McKinley after the fire and you don't see *me* disappearing like that mother of hers."

"Audrey is Julia's friend—"

"I don't care! I don't like them spending so much time together. That family is trouble . . ." Their voices faded as they walked back to the table.

Audrey waited several seconds before following them. She was starting to think she should turn around right now and walk out the diner's front door. Skip the carnival altogether and just go home.

But the thought that someone wanted to meet her at midnight kept her moving forward.

▶ 8 ◀

Harlow

HARLOW SET OUT FROM HER HOUSE AT THE
end of Hilltop Street just as the sun was setting. Like
many people in Clarkville, she had chosen to wear a
costume to the carnival, and she was pleased to see that
her black-and-white mask covered her entire face. With
her hair tucked up underneath the hot pink wig she was
also wearing, she could be anyone. Anyone, but hopefully not Harlow Carlson.

In the end, it was the note itself that had changed
her mind. *Come* to the carnival. *Meet me* at the Ferris

wheel. The language was vaguely taunting, like a dare.

Harlow never could resist a dare.

Once in the fourth grade, Ethan McKinley had dared her to eat one of the live crickets he fed to his pet snake. The cricket had wiggled in her mouth and tasted disgusting, but she'd eaten it anyway. It had been worth it to see the look on Ethan's face as she crunched her way through not one, not two, but *three* crickets. Harlow could face any dare because she wasn't afraid of anything—well, except for spiders, but thankfully Ethan hadn't asked her to eat any of *those*. Julia had once dared her to let a spider crawl up her arm; it was the only dare Harlow had ever turned down.

Another time when she was at the carnival, a friend— back when Harlow was still someone people wanted to be friends with—had dared her to ride the Fun Slide backward. She'd lain on her back staring up at the stars the whole way down. It had been such a great moment; she'd only wished she'd captured it with her camera.

After her mother left, Harlow had hunted through old trunks in the attic looking for a disguise. Besides the mask and wig, she'd found a black sheath that she'd draped over her jeans and sweater.

Just before she left she'd decided to put on some new leather boots her father brought back from his last business trip. She'd never worn them; she'd learned the hard way not to bring expensive items to school. But tonight she wasn't Harlow Carlson.

Tonight in her disguise she could be anyone she wanted.

Harlow may have been going to the carnival, but she doubted she'd stay till midnight. If one of her classmates wanted to speak to her so badly, they could track her down at school next week and say whatever it was they had to say straight to her face.

The sun sank lower, and the sky became soft and lavender. It was Harlow's favorite part of the day, when each moment seemed to hold magic . . . but all too soon, she knew, the purplish sky would turn dark and foreboding, the moon would rise, and strange things would come creeping out of the shadows.

Autumn leaves blew out of her path as she walked,

and the few that remained on the trees whispered as though they were gossiping to one another. The farther she went, the more crowded the street became with others making their way to the carnival. Three girls dressed in party dresses and gorilla masks walked in front of her. A girl fell in step beside her. Harlow glanced over and saw it was Erin Donoghue. Her spine stiffened; she was sort of mad about the spider incident earlier.

Harlow and Erin used to be friends; they ate at the same lunch table every day. Back when Harlow was the center of everyone's attention. Now Harlow sat alone at an empty table in the corner, shoveling food as fast as she could until, mercifully, she was finished and could escape to the library, where she could hide until the bell rang.

"Nice mask," Erin said.

"Uh, thanks," Harlow answered. Like Audrey and Julia, Erin was also wearing a tiara and a red feather boa, and Harlow realized that someone—well, *Julia*, obviously—had decided they should wear matching costumes tonight. Erin was also carrying a brown shoebox, which she held out carefully in front of her.

"What's your name?" Erin asked, and Harlow realized her costume had worked; Erin didn't recognize her.

"Um . . . it's Jean." Harlow didn't like to lie, but she felt that at certain times it was warranted, this occasion being one of them. Besides, *Jean* was the first name of the movie star Harlow had been named after, so she figured it wasn't a complete lie.

"Nice name," Erin said. "Are you from out of town?"

Harlow didn't know why Erin would think that, but being a stranger from out of town suited her just fine right now, so she said, "Sure." The mask plus the sore throat she was getting over made her voice sound muted and scratchy, like a raspy rock star's.

"What's in the box?" Harlow asked, and Erin shrugged.

"Nothing important," she answered.

They continued to walk. The wind kicked up and the air smelled of ash and broken things. Or maybe she just imagined it did.

"I hate walking around here," Erin said, shivering. "I hear it's haunted." She pointed to the old factory.

Nearly a year after the fire, the place was little more than a burned shell over a black stain on the ground. The only noticeable thing was the old sign, still visible at the entrance. Nasty graffiti covered it now, but the original greeting was still legible:

WELCOME TO THE CARLSON FACTORY.

"The factory burned down last year," Erin said, following Harlow's gaze. She dropped her voice and whispered. "It was terrible. People died."

Not people, Harlow wanted to correct her. *Only one person died that night. One man—and you barely knew him.*

"My uncle used to work there," Erin continued. "He lost his job that night."

The factory hadn't been terribly large, but Clarkville wasn't a terribly large town. And when the factory went up in flames, so did the jobs of nearly half the people in town. The Carlson Factory—the only factory in town—had made a small part that went into another part that was in many dishwashers. Harlow had never really understood it, exactly, but she did know that rebuilding the factory was proving difficult. There were a whole lot of places in the world where it was cheaper to make tiny dishwasher parts than in Clarkville, and many families in town were seriously struggling.

But, as Julia King liked to point out, Harlow and her family were rich—they had no idea what anyone else in town was going through. That's why few people at school talked to Harlow anymore—Julia had made sure of it.

The Monday after the fire Harlow had showed up to school with a brand-new iPhone. Julia said Harlow was being mean and insensitive. "How could you?" Julia said as soon as Harlow sat down at their usual lunch table and pulled out her phone to show everyone. "How could you flaunt that in front of us when half of our dads are out of a job now?" Julia had raised her voice, so almost everyone in the cafeteria heard her. Harlow had glanced around the room and saw Julia wasn't the only one who felt that way.

The embarrassing thing was she hadn't thought about it, not even once, that maybe bringing a brand-new phone to school that day was a bad idea. Three days after the fire, Harlow hadn't been thinking about much at all. She'd been numb. Her parents' factory was gone. Grace's dad was dead. Audrey's dad had just gotten out of the hospital—neither Audrey nor Grace were at school that day. When Harlow had taken her phone out of her backpack she'd been hoping both of them had texted her.

But from that day on it seemed the story was set: Harlow was rich and insensitive while most everyone else in town was struggling, and it was clear she wasn't welcome to sit with her old friends anymore. Julia took over Harlow's spot as their group's leader, and Harlow was left on her own.

The Carlsons may have had a lot of money, but they didn't have enough to single-handedly rebuild the factory on their own. That was why her father was working so hard to recruit investors; without them, the factory couldn't reopen.

Harlow was still staring at the graffitied sign, listening to Erin talk about all the bad things that had happened after the fire, when it occurred to her: Welcome baskets and spreadsheets don't tell a story. But *Harlow* knew how to tell a story. Wasn't she doing that already as the editor of the yearbook? Telling the story of the school, one photo at a time? And with all the extra pictures Mrs. Murphy had asked her to take, wasn't she already telling the story of Clarkville?

What if tomorrow morning, besides the proposal, the investors had another presentation to watch? One that told them the story of Clarkville—the amazing place that it was, and the amazing place it still could be one day. What if Harlow was the one to save Clarkville? Would that change the way everyone in school looked at her?

Harlow turned and began quickly walking; Erin practically had to jog to keep up with her long strides. She needed to get to the carnival as soon as possible.

9

Grace

6 HOURS TO MIDNIGHT

GRACE WAS STANDING IN FRONT OF THE iron gates twisting her ticket in her hands. The crowd milled around her; some dressed in costumes, some not. Beyond the gates she could see the carnival, brightly lit like a shining city set against the dusky sky. The air tasted of secrets and excitement, and the people around her were chattering. Because when it came to the Carnival of Wishes and Dreams, everyone had a story to tell.

Grace's own mother met Chrissy Schwartz—owner

of Schwartz Salon—at the carnival right after she'd ridden the carousel and wished to become a hair stylist. The other wish she'd made on the carousel was to fall in love. Two hours later, she'd met Grace's dad. Well, not exactly. Both Grace's parents had grown up in Clarkville and had known each other all their lives. But that year—their senior year of high school—they'd run into each other at the Ferris wheel and it was like they'd both been hit with a love spell. Her mother said it was one of the greatest nights of her life.

Grace wanted her own magical carnival story. Especially since she might spend the rest of her life grounded. Dread was pecking at her insides like pigeons with a stray bread crust. Her mother was going to *freak out* when she came home and saw Grace's note. What had she been thinking? She'd never sneaked out of the house before.

Lulu Pepperton was standing next to Grace, grumbling. "Why didn't they invite *me*? Julia *knows* how much I love banana splits." Lulu had cornered Grace the minute she arrived so they could examine the pictures Audrey kept posting online.

"I specifically *asked* Julia if she wanted to hang out before the carnival, and she said she was busy," Lulu continued. "Did Julia invite you?"

"I still haven't eaten dinner," Grace said, choosing her words carefully. As punctuation, Grace's stomach chose that exact moment to make a very loud and very long gurgling sound.

The loudspeakers crackled to life and a deep voice boomed, *"Ladies and gentlemen, may I direct your attention to the skies?"* Fireworks exploded into the night—popping, spinning, and whizzing in shades of red and gold and orange and silver. *"Welcome to the Carnival of Wishes and Dreams! Enjoy the night; may it be memorable and full of delight!"* A cheer went up from the crowd as the iron gates unlocked. Everyone began streaming inside, but Grace hesitated.

Her dad had loved the carnival. Together they had ridden every ride, visited every attraction. She hadn't been to this part of town since the fire. Across the field she could barely make out the burned remains of the Carlson Factory.

Thinking about the fire made Grace want to go home, except right then she caught a glimpse of the Ferris wheel, rising up above the rest of the carnival like a multicolored moon. It had been her and her dad's favorite ride. She placed her hand on her jeans pocket, where she'd stuffed her pumpkin gram, and couldn't help but wonder what she'd find at midnight. Who would be waiting for her?

At the end of the night, would she have her own magical carnival story to tell?

"Grace! Lulu!" The two of them turned and saw Julia approaching, Audrey following along behind.

"Where have you guys *been*?" Julia said as though *she* was the one who'd been waiting near the entrance for the last half hour.

"How was dinner?" Lulu asked, and Julia waved her hand.

"Totally boring," she said.

"It didn't *look* boring," Lulu mumbled.

Audrey and Grace smiled politely at each other but

said nothing. Grace wasn't supposed to hang out with Audrey anymore, but it was kind of difficult when they still had the same friends.

"I thought you couldn't come because you're grounded?" Julia said to Grace.

"She sneaked out of the house!" Lulu squealed. "Can you believe it?"

"How long can you stay?" Julia asked.

"Until I feel like leaving," Grace answered. She didn't add that she definitely wouldn't feel like leaving before the early hours of tomorrow morning. She was keeping her midnight appointment at the Ferris wheel a secret.

Everyone congratulated Grace on her new status as a curfew-breaking troublemaker, and then Julia frowned and said, "Why aren't you wearing your tiara?"

"I *am* wearing it," Grace said. "See?" She took off her baseball hat and showed them the tiara, which was underneath. No way was she trading in her lucky Cubs cap on her last night in Clarkville. Not for a stupid tiara.

"Julia! Julia! Wait up!" Erin pushed her way into their group, expertly edging between Julia and Audrey. "I met the coolest girl on the walk over," Erin was saying. "She's really tall—I think she's in high school—she has the *best* boots."

They walked deeper into the carnival. Everywhere Grace looked there were blinking lights, laughing faces, and the striped red-and-gold flags of the carnival flapping over the tops of game and snack stands. Jugglers, puppeteers, and mimes with painted white faces wove through the crowd, and a pair of stilt walkers teetered dangerously close to a man puffing flames into the night. Grace was so caught up in the sights she barely heard Erin lean closer to Julia and whisper, "It's done."

"Step right up!" a game vendor called out to Grace. "Knock down these milk bottles and get a prize. Four in a row wins a Clarkville High baseball jersey."

"Thanks," Grace called back, "but I already have one of those." It was true; she had her dad's old baseball jersey, which she sometimes slept in. He'd also given her his trophies and his old mitt—everything he treasured from his high school days. Everything, that is, except his state championship ring, which he'd always worn on his right hand. Grace swallowed; the ring had somehow gotten lost the night of the fire.

Julia detached herself from Erin and slipped back to talk to Grace. "Did your mom pick you and Diego up from school today?" she asked.

Grace shook her head. "Diego's dad did," she answered. Their families only lived a few streets away, and for the last year Grace's mom and Mr. Martinez took turns driving her and Diego home from school. Getting to sit next to him was the best part of the day, even if she could rarely bring herself to speak to him.

Grace pulled her phone out. She checked the time and tried to decide just how long she had left before her mother returned home.

"So, did he say anything to you?" Julia asked.

"About what?" Grace said. She looked up and saw Miss Miller from her mom's book club, and her heart nearly stopped. The meeting couldn't be over already, could it?

"About *me*, Grace," Julia said, clearly irritated. "About the pumpkin gram I gave him."

"Oh, right." Grace shoved her phone back in her pocket. "No—but he probably couldn't, though, not with his dad in the car."

That was all true; his dad *had* been whistling loudly off-key, and it had been an uncomfortable car ride. Especially since Grace still had the impression Diego had wanted to say something to her. But none of that was the reason why he hadn't mentioned the pumpkin gram from Julia.

The real reason was that Diego had never actually received the pumpkin gram from Julia. Grace had destroyed it before it ever reached Diego. It was another one of the very bad things she had done.

Grace didn't know what had come over her. Julia had been in a hurry yesterday when they bought their pumpkin grams, and she'd suddenly remembered a few extras she'd needed to purchase before the bell rang. She'd shoved the ones she'd already written into Grace's hands and asked her to turn them into the box the student government had set up in the cafeteria.

Grace hadn't meant to read Julia's messages. She

really hadn't. But she saw Diego's name printed in Julia's neat handwriting and she couldn't stop herself from taking a peek: *Hey, Diego! Want to meet up at the carnival? XXXOOOXXX*

It was all the Xs and Os that did it.

Grace had promptly dropped the other pumpkin grams in the box, and tossed Diego's into the trash. It was like temporary insanity. She didn't think; she just acted, and couldn't be held responsible for her actions. She just knew that with that pumpkin gram Julia was trying to claim Diego, just like she had claimed the best seat in the cafeteria.

Julia shouldn't get to have Diego, the boy Grace had loved since forever. So she destroyed the pumpkin gram.

And now she was terrified Julia and the others would find out.

It wasn't like she could actually *tell* Julia they had a crush on the same boy. That was a quick way to get on Julia's bad side. Being on Julia King's bad side was a place you did not want to be. Currently Harlow Carlson occupied the top spot on Julia's bad side. It was possible

Grace was *already* on Julia's bad side and just didn't know it yet. That could happen. Poor Audrey still thought Julia was her best friend.

"Do you think I should say something to Diego?" Julia asked.

"Ummm . . . ," Grace began.

"Hey, you guys!" Erin called. "The line for the Fun Slide is already getting long. Let's go on it now before it gets even longer."

"Okay!" Julia called back. Then she whispered to Grace, "Maybe later we can go find Diego."

"Sure," Grace whispered miserably.

At least there was one bright side, Grace thought to herself as they joined the line for the Fun Slide. Maybe Julia would be so distracted hunting for Diego, she'd forget what she was planning to do to Harlow tonight.

10

Harlow

THE REGULAR EMPLOYEES OF THE CARNIVAL—
the carnies, as everyone called them—traveled around
the state with the rides and had a reputation for being
a rough bunch. The carnie standing in front of the
iron gates had greasy hair, a thick scar slithering up his
arm, and a smile that looked more like a grimace as he
greeted Harlow. "Welcome to the Carnival of Wishes
and Dreams! May I take your ticket?"

Harlow felt around in her pocket and handed it
over. The ticket was red, and in shiny gold letters it

said **ADMIT ONE**. In that moment Harlow keenly felt that she was *one*, and for a few painful seconds wished she had someone to walk with into the carnival. She almost wished she hadn't let herself get separated from Erin as they approached the iron gates. Erin had sprinted ahead, saying she needed to do something before she met her friends, and since Harlow had been afraid Erin would discover her true identity anyway, she'd hung back.

But maybe if she helped her parents reopen the factory, she could get some of her friends back. Or, at the very least, maybe everyone would stop hating her.

As soon as she stepped past the iron gates she was mesmerized, like she was every year, by the bright colors, the blinking lights, and the smells of hot buttered popcorn and roasted peanuts.

She walked around taking candid shots—capturing moments—with the camera on her phone. Over at the Kissing Booth, she snapped a picture of her teacher Miss Prescott smooching her boyfriend. Harlow smirked; too bad she couldn't put *that one* in the yearbook. She also snapped a picture of Ethan McKinley and his best friend, Travis McManus, getting yelled at by a carnie after the two of them tried cutting to the front of the Tilt-A-Whirl line. She stood practically right in front of them, and they didn't recognize her.

After she thought she had enough candid photos, she set her phone to the video setting and looked around. Pictures were one thing, but she also needed to get some interviews. She saw old Mr. Tolland leaning on his cane while he watched his grandchildren ride the Zipper. She figured he'd be a great first choice for an interview; he'd retired a few years ago, but before that he'd worked for the factory since before her father was even born, back when Harlow's grandfather ran everything.

"Hi, Mr. Tolland," she said, holding up her phone. "I was wondering if I could get a video of you?"

Mr. Tolland leaned on his cane and squinted at her suspiciously. "Who are you? You're not going to put me on the YouTube, are you?"

Harlow removed her mask and said, "It's *me*, sir. Harlow, Russ Carlson's daughter."

"Oh, Harlow!" he said, breaking into a grin. "What can I do for you?"

"Did you know my dad is bringing in some potential investors tonight?" she asked, and he nodded.

"Everyone in town's been talking about it," he said.

"I bet," Harlow answered. "Anyway, I'm putting together a video presentation, and I was wondering if you would mind telling me—on camera—what makes Clarkville so special?"

Mr. Tolland's eyes lit up. "That's a fine idea, Harlow. I'd be happy to help. Just say the word." Harlow held up her phone and centered the camera. When she gave a thumbs-up, Mr. Tolland said, "Clarkville is special because it's home. My family has lived here for generations. My own grandfather grew up farming the soil. . . ."

He spoke for nearly ten minutes, his white hair blowing in the breeze, even after his grandkids joined him and it was clear they'd rather go on another ride. "Clarkville is a wonderful place," he finished, and, glaring at the camera, added, "and if you had any sense in those

East Coast heads of yours, you'd see that." He looked over at Harlow. "How was that?" he asked.

"Great," she answered, although she was definitely going to have to cut out that last part. "Thank you."

"That's a cool mask," one of Mr. Tolland's grandkids said. "Can you see out of it?"

"Yeah. See?" Harlow slipped the mask back on and blinked at them.

They left to go on another ride, and Harlow wandered around, replaying Mr. Tolland's interview as she walked. She was so engrossed in the video that she didn't hear Erin calling "Jean!" until she'd nearly walked right into her. Erin wasn't alone; she was with Julia, Audrey, Lulu, and Grace. They were all wearing red feather boas and tiaras. Julia's tiara appeared to be made of crystals and glittered when it caught the light. Harlow swallowed and wondered if any of them would recognize her.

"Hello!" Erin said. "Remember me?" She turned to Julia. "This is the girl I told you about with the cute boots. Her name's Jean." She turned back to Harlow.

"We just got off the Fun Slide and we're heading over to the Tilt-A-Whirl—want to join us?"

"Um . . ." Harlow knew she should keep working on her project. It would take her awhile to get all of the interviews and even more time to put together the presentation. But the idea of accepting a freely given invitation sounded nice, even though she realized her costume had worked: Erin and the others had no idea who she was. If they could see her real face, they'd walk away, guaranteed.

"Are you in?" Erin said.

"I'm in," Harlow said, promising herself she'd get back to her video project soon. For just a little while, she wanted to pretend she had friends again.

Is there anything as exciting as patrolling the perimeter of a carnival with your friends on a giddy Friday night, searching for the boy you like?

Harlow wasn't so sure herself—the last big crush she had was on Ethan McKinley over a year ago, and she never told anyone because she thought Audrey might not approve. She hadn't had a crush on anyone since. But Grace had always had a crush on Diego, and judging by the pinched look on her face, she still did, and wasn't happy that he was Julia's latest flavor of the week.

After they'd ridden the Tilt-A-Whirl Julia said she wanted to wander around the carnival. At first Harlow had been glad; she'd spent the entire ride with her hands clamped down against her mask and wig, hoping neither would fly off. She wasn't in any hurry to get on another ride, but it quickly became apparent that Julia was in a hurry. To find Diego.

Harlow glanced again at Grace's unhappy face and wished she could console her old friend. Julia would probably like someone else next week; she changed crushes as often as other people changed socks.

But then Harlow remembered Grace didn't have another week. She was moving tomorrow. Harlow wanted so badly to say goodbye to Grace. Instead, maybe she could give her a small farewell present.

"Any chance we could stop walking for a bit?"

Harlow asked, tapping at her boots. "My feet are killing me."

"Where *did* you get your boots, Jean?" Julia asked, coming to a halt. "I love them."

"In Chicago," Harlow answered. "I live there," she added, just to be safe.

"Julia is taking two people to Chicago for her birthday," Lulu put in. She turned to Julia. "Any idea who you're taking?"

Julia shrugged. "Haven't decided yet."

From there the conversation turned to shoes, clothes, and music. Harlow felt her uneasiness leaking away. Her disguise was working, and everyone seemed to really like "Jean."

"I'm getting tired of just standing around," Audrey said suddenly. "The bumper cars are just up ahead—let's go ride them. Last one there is a rotten egg!"

She took off running and everyone except Harlow and Julia ran after her. Harlow couldn't run. She hadn't been lying; her feet really were killing her. Wearing the boots tonight hadn't been a smart idea.

"I don't see what's so exciting about the bumper cars," Julia grumbled to Harlow. "It's a stupid ride," she added, but Harlow was pretty sure Julia was just mad they'd all run off without consulting her first. She had forgotten Julia could be like that sometimes.

"Julia!" Mrs. King came striding up to them. "I've been looking for you everywhere. Why didn't you answer my text?"

Julia batted her eyes innocently, "Oh, did you text me?"

"You know I did." She paused as her gaze drifted to Harlow. "Who's your friend?" she asked.

"This is Jean. We just met her tonight—she's from Chicago."

"Nice to meet you, Jean." Mrs. King turned her attention back to Julia and sighed. "Your dad and I have been talking, and . . ." She took a deep breath. "I'm sorry—but we're going to have to cancel the trip to the city next weekend."

"You mean my birthday party? But last night you said I could take two people!"

"I said *maybe* you could take two people. Your dad

and I have been talking tonight, and as much as we want to, we just can't swing it this year."

Julia looked outraged. "But I already texted my friends!"

"Well, you shouldn't have. I specifically told you *not* to text them yet. You're just going to have to tell them we'll come up with another plan that's more doable. I'm sorry, but that's the way things need to be this year."

Mrs. King walked away after that and Julia looked at the ground. Harlow saw a couple of tears roll down her cheeks. "Are you okay?" she asked.

"I'm fine," Julia answered. She turned away quickly and wiped her eyes. "It's stupid, but . . . I had this dream of getting out of a fancy car wearing a party dress—I saved up money and bought a sparkly pink one—and then walking into a beautiful building." She glanced at Harlow. "It's stupid, I know."

"It's not stupid," Harlow said. She dreamed of things like that herself sometimes. Of sparkling, glittering moments—when everything is festive and everyone is happy. Sure, Julia would have taken a ton of selfies and posted the moment online for everyone to see, but so what? Didn't everyone have secret wishes and dreams they might be embarrassed to tell anyone about, but desperately hoped would come true?

"Are you mad?" Harlow asked.

"At my parents?" Julia said, wiping her eyes again. "Yes. No—I don't know. I should have just told them I didn't want a birthday party this year; it would have been easier on them. My dad used to work at a factory and he lost his job last year—it's a long story—and things have been tough. My parents almost lost our house."

"Lost?" Harlow repeated. *How do you lose a house?* she wanted to ask. She pictured the Kings' residence—a redbrick colonial—racing down the street like a puppy suddenly let off his leash.

"Well, not lost," Julia said, as though she could read Harlow's mind. "Foreclosed."

"Oh . . ." Harlow let the word out in one long breath, because she knew what it meant. Foreclosure—that meant the Kings had been having trouble making their mortgage payments, and if they missed too many, the bank would take their house away from them. That's what happened to Audrey's family last spring.

"Anyway," Julia continued, "my mom started selling houses and things are a little better now, but . . ." She shrugged. "Things happen, right?"

"Yes," Harlow agreed. Things *did* happen. Awful things, like fires and losing parents and houses. But hopeful things still happened too. Like standing with an old friend in the middle of the Carnival of Wishes and Dreams and talking about something that really mattered.

Harlow wished she could capture the moment with her camera. Instead she settled for staring at Julia as she spoke. It was like getting a glimpse behind the curtain. Behind the shiny images Julia always posted online—the ones that made it seem like her whole life was just one big party.

"Can you do me a favor?" Julia said, and Harlow nodded. "Can you keep this a secret? I don't feel like dealing with this tonight. I'll tell my friends the party is canceled on Monday."

"Sure," Harlow said. "I'm sure they'll understand. . . . Maybe next weekend you could do something else for your birthday," she added. "Maybe instead of your party we could throw a sleepover. I could help you."

Julia glanced at her strangely. "Won't you be back in Chicago next weekend?"

Just like that, the moment vanished. Julia wasn't confiding in *Harlow*, but in Jean. And Jean was nothing. A phantom who would vanish forever the instant Harlow took off her costume and made her way back to her lonely house on Hilltop Street.

Harlow tugged at the edge of her mask. Maybe it was time to take it off and come clean. Tell Julia that even if she didn't exactly understand what everyone else in town was going through, she was trying hard tonight with her video project to make things better for everyone.

But Julia was already moving toward the bumper cars, her usual cool expression on her face, and Harlow understood that her peek behind the curtain was over.

11

Audrey

5 HOURS TO MIDNIGHT

AUDREY STOOD IN LINE, FRUSTRATED, WHILE her friends chatted behind her. She didn't even *like* the bumper cars; she'd only suggested they ride them because she'd suddenly noticed Diego passing nearby with his friends and she didn't want Julia to see. Audrey and Grace weren't really friends anymore—but that didn't mean she'd forgotten about Grace's epic crush on Diego. She'd thought if she could keep Julia from noticing him maybe she could save Grace a little heartache tonight.

But her plan hadn't even worked. Julia and that girl Jean had lingered behind. As Audrey watched, Diego got in line across the way for the Zipper and Julia and Jean were stopped by Mrs. King. Hopefully Julia would be too preoccupied to notice Diego. But even if she did, Audrey had a much bigger problem:

Her father still hadn't arrived at the carnival.

While they'd walked around looking for Diego they'd passed the Ferris wheel, and an irritated-looking carnie was manning the controls instead of her father. As she stood in line for the bumper cars Audrey wondered if she should leave the carnival and go home. What if he had fallen asleep after she'd left?

"Who do you think she's going to take to the city?" Lulu was saying. Behind Audrey, Erin and Lulu were using Julia's temporary absence to discuss her birthday party while Grace just looked on silently, as usual.

Audrey ignored everyone. She leaned away from the others and quickly called her dad. It went straight to voice mail. "Dad," she said quietly. "I'm at the carnival. Where are you? Call me back."

She hung up and wished for the millionth time her mother was here. *She* would know what to do. Her father needed to show up tonight for his shift. They really needed the extra money, and no matter how many times her father told her not to worry, Audrey did anyway. *Someone* had to worry.

While she waited, she decided to post another picture online. She'd already posted two since arriving at the carnival. One of her and Julia standing in front of the iron gates and one of the Curiosity Shoppe—a tented store that sold creepy candy and insects and other weird odds and ends. She'd gotten a lot of likes, but not any new followers. She turned her camera around and snapped a selfie, then examined the picture. It wasn't a bad shot. She was supposed to send in a head shot along with her online audition for *Middle School Daze*. She couldn't afford to get professional head shots done—maybe a couple of really good selfies would work?

Just then her phone pinged—someone had followed her. Now she had two hundred ninety-nine followers! She was one ahead of Julia and one away from her goal.

The line suddenly surged forward. They entered the track and Audrey claimed a bumper car—a blue-and-white-striped one near the front. Grace got into a car next to her, and Erin and Lulu climbed into a red one together. Jean and Julia came rushing in; they were the last two let inside, and Jean quickly hopped in next to Grace.

"Over here!" Audrey waved to Julia. Julia didn't seem to see or hear her; she squeezed into Lulu and Erin's car at the last second, pushing Erin into the middle so she could drive.

Audrey stepped on the gas pedal, but her car stubbornly refused to move. She muttered a word that tastes like soap in your mouth and the car—seemingly shocked by her soapy language—shot forward. Audrey's arm jerked the steering wheel and she nearly drove into the perimeter barrier. But then she righted herself and joined the flow of other cars.

Or tried to, anyway. From behind she felt a sudden *thwack!* She turned her head; Grace and Jean had slammed their car into hers. "Hi, Audrey!" Jean waved playfully and then they were off, gunning their car toward their next target.

Audrey's car was slower to recover, and by the time it was finally moving forward another *thwack!* came from the side, this time from Julia, Erin, and Lulu's car. "Hi!" Audrey said, trying to sound cheerful. But the other three didn't seem to have heard her. While her car stalled, getting pushed and slammed this way and that, Julia, Lulu, and Erin's car shot around the track, expertly dodging the other cars until Julia gunned it straight into the side of Audrey's car.

"Hey!" Audrey cried, as her car stalled a second time. "Lay off, will you?"

Once again, her friends didn't seem to have heard. Or maybe they were just ignoring her.

They definitely weren't ignoring her bumper car, though. While she was stuck in the middle of the track, her car shuddering and sputtering, Julia kept running into her. One time she rammed Audrey's car so hard it went flying straight into the barrier perimeter. Just as she was trying to right her car and head back into the flow of traffic, her gaze strayed to the crowd passing by and settled on a woman wearing a pirate costume.

For the briefest flash of a second—before the woman was swallowed by the lights and the crowd—Audrey thought she saw her mother.

"Wake up, Audrey!" Erin said as they rammed their car into Audrey's yet again.

Audrey shook herself, certain she'd only imagined it was her mother's face she'd seen, and tried to get her car moving. It was a lost cause, though, because all the cars were coming to a halt. The ride had ended.

Audrey climbed out of her car and exited the ride behind Julia, who had thrown an arm around both Erin and Lulu and left without a backward glance at Audrey. As she followed them she couldn't help but wonder: Was Julia mad at her?

▶ 12 ◀

Grace

GRACE COULDN'T DECIDE IF HER MAGICAL carnival story was turning into a comedy or a tragedy. Julia had dragged them all around the carnival grounds searching for Diego, Grace's heart hammering the whole time. Then, just when Diego appeared and it seemed like they were about to run right into him, Audrey had suddenly led them over to the bumper cars.

Grace was grateful no one else had noticed Diego, but now she was starting to wish the night—her last night in Clarkville—wasn't flying by so quickly.

"Where should we go next?" Lulu asked as they were all leaving the bumper cars.

"Let's get funnel cakes," Grace said, her stomach rumbling, just as Erin answered, "Let's go on another ride—before the lines get too long." Then everyone looked to Julia to make the final decision.

"Erin's right," Julia said. "The lines are getting long. . . . Audrey, can you do me a favor and go get Grace a funnel cake while we wait in line?"

"Audrey doesn't have to—" Grace began.

"Sure," Audrey said. She looked distracted and eager to leave for some reason, but still, Grace rolled her eyes anyway. Julia had a habit of sending them on errands. Usually she sent Lulu or Erin, but lately it seemed to Grace that Julia had been treating Audrey like her own personal assistant. And anyway, it wasn't like Grace wasn't capable of buying her own dinner.

Grace was just about to say exactly that when she caught the faint sound of an organ playing a slow, melancholy tune. It was the music of the carousel, the one that some people swore could grant wishes. Grace figured a little wishing magic might change her night for the better.

"Actually, let's go on the carousel next. I want to make a wish." Grace turned to Audrey. "And I think you should ride with us." She turned back and began walking. Everyone was so startled Grace had spoken up and made a decision that they followed her.

"The carousel doesn't *really* grant wishes," Julia huffed as she fell into step beside Grace, regaining her usual place at the front of their group.

"Yeah," Lulu echoed. "Carousels are dumb."

As they walked, Jean began chatting with Erin and Julia about a TV show it turned out they all liked. There was something odd about that girl. Something Grace couldn't quite put her finger on.

She kept following the music; the brightly lit carousel was placed at the back of the carnival. A light fog was descending on the wheat field beyond, giving everything an eerie orange glow. At the top of the carousel, golden tragedy faces looked down over gilded oval mirrors, laughing and leering at the crowd below. Grace shivered. Was it her imagination, or had the temperature dropped suddenly?

"What are you wishing for, Grace?" Lulu asked as they took their place in line.

"That living in California won't completely suck," Grace answered, but she was lying.

"I've been to California," Jean spoke up. "It's awesome. People go there for vacation—and you'll get to *live* there. Think about how awful winters are in Clarkville." Jean's voice was raspy, but there was something familiar about her. Plus, wasn't she from out of town? How did she know about winter in Clarkville?

"Well, *I* believe the carousel can grant wishes," Erin said, "so I'm making as many as I can think of."

Everyone fell silent as they waited, pondering all the wishes they could make.

It was just folklore, Grace was sure, but there *were* a handful of people in Clarkville who swore they'd made a wish while riding the carousel, only to have it come true afterward. Besides her mother, Mrs. Pearson—the bus driver—swore up and down she'd wished she could take her daughter to see her favorite band in concert. Then a little while later, she found two tickets lying in the grass.

But how exactly was it all supposed to work? Grace wondered as the line began moving forward. Did she make a wish at the end of the ride? Did she wish now? Grace wanted her magical carnival story; she didn't want to take any chances. She had a list of wishes ready to go. The minute she stepped onto the carousel she quickly whispered each one:

I wish that my mother won't find me tonight so I can make it to the Ferris wheel at midnight.

I wish I could find my dad's missing baseball ring.

I wish I didn't have to move to California.

I wish that nothing bad will happen to Harlow Carlson tonight.

I wish Diego Martinez would kiss me at the carnival.

The last one was something she would be too embarrassed to tell anyone. But she had this picture in her mind: Kissing the boy she'd always loved, the carnival lights flaring and flashing all around them, on her last night in Clarkville.

13

Harlow

HARLOW WOVE THROUGH THE BRASS poles and hurried to the fiercest and strongest wooden horse she could find, a white stallion with a large black mane that looked ready to break free from the carousel and go running into the foggy wheat field beyond the carnival gates.

Things were looking up! Erin and Julia seemed to really like "Jean." The whole time they stood in line they'd talked about a show they liked on TV and a boy in Erin's English class she had a crush on. Harlow had even managed to snap a couple great photos of the carousel that she was definitely putting in her presentation.

"Hi, Jean!" Julia and Erin claimed horses on Harlow's right and left, and the three of them took turns taking selfies while they waited for the ride to start. Harlow examined their shining faces and was struck by a burst of inspiration.

She turned to Julia. "Hey, can you help me with a school project I'm doing?" She held up her camera. "Can I make a short video of you telling me why you like Clarkville?"

Julia—who loved being on camera—didn't seem to think it was an odd request. "Sure!" she said. After Harlow started filming with her phone, Julia said, "I love Clarkville because . . ." She glanced around at the carousel and said, "Because it's the place where dreams come true!" She giggled and Harlow stopped filming. Perfect. That one was definitely going into the presentation.

A few seconds later Erin leaned over and whispered, "There he is!"

"Who?" Harlow said.

"The guy I was telling you about? The one in my English class? He's over there, eating a candy apple." Erin pointed—right at Lucas Carter, the boy who'd handed Harlow the unsigned pumpkin gram earlier that day.

"Oh, he's—" Harlow stopped herself. She'd been about to say, "He's in my Spanish class—he's really nice!" But of course she couldn't say that. "Jean" didn't go to Clarkville Middle School. "He's really cute," she said finally.

The music started up; the horses began to rise and the carousel began to spin. Harlow hadn't planned on making any wishes—she didn't believe there was anything special about the carousel—but now the whole night seemed to be crackling with possibility and she thought, *Why not?* A little wishing and dreaming never hurt anyone:

I wish the factory would get rebuilt.

I wish I could get my friends back.

Maybe sometime very soon she would reveal her true identity. As the carousel spun around she imagined a touching scene where she would take her mask off and say to everyone, "I've missed you all." The girls would be surprised and amazed, but Julia, clearly moved that Harlow had kept her secret when she confided about the canceled birthday party, would say, "I've missed you too." Why not wish for it to happen just like that? And while she was at it, she had one other wish:

I wish someone wonderful will be waiting for me at the Ferris wheel at midnight.

She was starting to change her mind about the anonymous pumpkin gram. The way the night was going, anything in the world seemed possible. Why *couldn't* someone wonderful be waiting for her at the Ferris wheel? She was willing to find out.

She was definitely staying till midnight.

14

Audrey

THE CAROUSEL CAME TO A STOP, AND Audrey knew she'd missed her chance. She really wanted to believe in magic. She liked to think there was magic in everyday things like dust motes and twinkle lights and lavender sunsets and autumn leaves. So when the ride had started up, she'd had every intention of making a wish. But then she'd started thinking about all the wishes she'd made over the last year. Not one of them had come true.

What was the point of even pretending to wish

when you knew it was all pointless anyway?

She watched as Julia and the others exited the ride, feeling strangely separate from everyone. Didn't any of them notice she was still sitting on her wooden horse?

The carnie operating the controls didn't seem to notice. He opened the metal gate holding back the line and with a lazy wave beckoned the crowd forward. Audrey stayed where she was, still as mouse, as the ride filled.

The music started and the carousel began to spin again. Audrey looked up and through the fog she glimpsed a star shooting across the night sky. For one wonderful second it seemed as though her horse was chasing after the stardust. Maybe the carousel plus the star would make her doubly lucky. She figured you were only supposed to make one wish per shooting star. But when you're down on your luck, you can't afford to be frugal, so she made five:

I wish my mom would come back.

I wish I'd get the lead in Middle School Daze.

► 15 ◄

Harlow

HARLOW'S MASK WAS STICKY WITH SWEAT and her wig itched the back of her neck, but she didn't care. The night just kept getting better and better! After the carousel they—well, *Julia*—decided they'd ride the Clown Faces next. Everyone—except for Audrey, whom Harlow figured had left to buy Grace's funnel cake—was laughing and talking as they made their way through the carnival, and Harlow was in the middle of it all!

She took a couple selfies with everyone and studied the photo. Her black-and-white mask looked slightly eerie among everyone else's tiaras and feather boas, but she didn't care—maybe she'd even put one of them into the yearbook. It could be a reminder of the night she got her friends back.

Harlow loved the Clown Faces; they reminded her of the teacup ride at Disneyland. Except instead of teacups, people crammed into a spinning top painted on the outside to look like a clown face. It spun round and round until you were so dizzy you wanted to puke your guts out. Harlow loved it.

It seemed a lot of other students from Clarkville Middle School loved it too. The line was really long, but Julia began pushing her way forward past several of their classmates, shouting, "Make way! Grace Chang wants to ride."

Harlow saw Grace frown, and she was pretty sure in that moment they were both feeling the same way: Grace wasn't *disabled*, after all. She didn't deserve to go to the front of the line just because her dad had died. But Julia seemed to think that was exactly what she— what *they*—deserved. Harlow felt an uncomfortable pit open up in her stomach. Julia had always been a little bossy, but this was way different.

"Move," Julia said when they came up to Ethan McKinley and his friends. "Grace wants to ride."

"So what?" Ethan said. He blocked their way, and Harlow had to stifle a giggle.

Ethan, who had apparently heard her, turned to her and said, "Who are you?"

"Who are *you*?" Harlow retorted, and everyone laughed. She had forgotten how nice it felt to have people laugh with her. To be part of a moment instead of merely capturing it through the lens of a camera.

"This is Jean," Julia said to Ethan. "We just met her tonight."

"Nice mask," Ethan said. "Why don't you take it off?"

Everyone turned to Harlow expectantly. She should have seen this coming. *Of course* they'd want her to take the mask off and see who she really was underneath.

The thing was, she oftentimes felt like her *own face* was a mask. The kids at school just saw her outside; they didn't see the girl she really was on the inside. Granted, most days Harlow didn't actually *know* who she really was on the inside, but she knew she wasn't the terrible person many of them thought she was.

She also knew the night would be over if she took off her mask.

"I can't take it off," Harlow said.

"Why not?" Ethan crossed his arms. "Why don't you want anyone to see your face? What are you, a ghost under there or something?"

"Yes," Harlow said, thinking fast, "and if you're not careful, I'll haunt you!"

Everyone laughed again, and the moment passed. It was nice to have Ethan look right at her. At school he always ignored her. Back when Harlow, Audrey, and Grace had sleepovers at the McKinleys' house, Ethan always hung out with them. Harlow missed those days. She and Ethan would constantly dare each other to do crazy things. The best one was when they dared each other to climb the really tall sycamore tree in the McKinleys' backyard. Afterward, Ethan had said something to her that she'd never told anyone—not even Audrey.

"Hey—have any of you seen my dad tonight?" Ethan said suddenly.

"No, why?" Erin asked.

Ethan shrugged and looked away. "No reason."

Just then Ethan's best friend—Travis McManus—joined them in line. He was carrying two plates of chili fries.

"Get those away from us," Erin said, wrinkling her nose. "They smell disgusting."

Travis shrugged. "Then get out of line." He held out a plate to Ethan. "Dude, here you go."

"*Dude*," Ethan said, pushing them away. "I'm not eating those right before we go on the Clown Faces."

And because it had always been so much fun to tease Ethan, Harlow spoke up and said, "Why not? Afraid you'll be sick on the ride?"

"No," Ethan said. "I just—"

"'Cause I totally understand if you are," Harlow continued. "Those chili fries look really tough. I wouldn't want to go up against them, either. I bet you'd puke them right up." Harlow smiled. Her mask was giving her a new boldness tonight. Or not new, exactly. Forgotten, maybe.

"I bet I wouldn't," Ethan said.

Harlow shrugged. "So eat them . . . *I dare you*," she couldn't resist adding.

"Fine, then." He held the chili fries out. "But you first."

She was about to snatch them when she realized she couldn't eat anything without taking her mask off.

"Next time," she said.

"Chicken," Ethan retorted, and Harlow was tempted to rip off her mask right then and there.

"Not hungry," she countered. "Besides, I'm right— you *will* puke them up."

"Oh yeah? Challenge accepted," Ethan said, and began shoving them into his mouth.

The line surged forward and Ethan had just enough time to finish scarfing down the chili fries before they all piled into the same clown face. A carnie came around to check their ride was secure before heading back to his control post.

The ride started up with a jerk; round and round they went, going faster and faster, until Harlow began to feel woozy and everyone seemed to swirl together in a tangle of arms and elbows and tiaras and laughing faces. Until it seemed they were one giant herd, unable to distinguish any one individual person.

This is what she had missed all year—being a part of something. Harlow wondered if her carousel wish would come true and she could get her friends back tonight.

All of a sudden, there was a loud *thump!* and the ride came to a juddering stop. Harlow and Ethan's knees knocked together, and Ethan made a slight retching sound. He was sweating, and his skin had taken on a greenish sheen.

"Sick yet?" Harlow said. She herself felt dizzy.

"No," Ethan answered quickly.

Over at the control post, the carnie was furiously punching at the gears. "Remain seated!" he called to everyone. "We'll have this fixed in no time."

"These rides are always breaking down," Julia complained. "It's a wonder anyone hasn't gotten hurt."

"Look," Lulu said suddenly, gesturing at the crowd passing by the ride. "It's Mr. Carlson."

Harlow glanced over and saw her father leading a long line of smartly dressed businesspeople toward the Snack Emporium. Harlow wondered if any of them realized an entire town was pinning their wishes and dreams on them.

"My mom says he'll never get the factory rebuilt," Julia said quietly. She was looking down at her hands, but Harlow had the feeling that if she could see Julia's eyes there'd be tears in them.

"The factory—" Harlow began, but quickly shut her mouth. "Jean" wouldn't know anything at all about any of this. "What factory?" she said instead.

"The one we walked by earlier, remember? I told you about it?" Erin said. "The Carlson Factory. Last year when it burned down, someone died in the building"—Erin glanced quickly at Grace, who'd gone very still—"a . . . um . . . firefighter who was there that night." Everyone was silent for a moment, seemingly out of respect for Grace, who, as usual, was staring off into space and saying nothing. Ethan and Julia were also saying nothing. Ethan was scowling and Julia was still looking at her hands. And Erin, who seemed like she was regretting bringing the subject up, suddenly said, "Hey, you guys, want to see a picture of Harlow Carlson?"

"What?" Harlow said, taken aback.

"Harlow Carlson, the factory owner's daughter—See, that's her!"

Erin held out her phone and Harlow's breath caught. It was a picture of her in Miss Prescott's class, wearing the clothes she'd worn to school that day. The picture must have been taken earlier that afternoon, and it was awful. Harlow was gazing out the classroom window. Her eyes were strangely blank. Her mouth was slack and parted slightly and her hand was raised, her finger poised near her nose like she was just about to pick it.

"Not her best look," Julia said.

"Yeah, she looks like she's drooling!" Lulu said.

"When did you take this?" Grace said, looking back up at Erin. She, at least, had the decency to sound disapproving.

"In math class today," Erin said.

Later, Harlow would think that if she'd spent more time with Erin this past year she'd have recognized the warning signs and been able to stop it. She would have seen Erin tapping and swiping on her phone and knew what it meant.

Grace, who *had* spent a lot of time with Erin this year, was quicker on the draw. "No, Erin, don't—" she began, but it was too late.

"Posted!" Erin held her phone up triumphantly. "Now *everyone* can see it!"

"Oh, Erin, you *didn't*!" Lulu whipped out her own phone and began scrolling.

Harlow breathed deep and willed herself to stay quiet. She had to leave, *now*. She couldn't spend one more second here.

Julia, who already seemed bored with the whole conversation, said, "When do you think the ride will get fixed? It's cramped in here."

In answer, Ethan leaned over the side and puked up his chili fries.

▶ 16 ◀

Audrey

4 HOURS TO MIDNIGHT

THE LINE FOR FUNNEL CAKES WASN'T THAT long, but it would have to wait.

Audrey passed the Snack Emporium and headed toward the Ferris wheel. "Please be there," she whispered under her breath. She glanced briefly at a girl wearing a vampire costume and sighed. She felt like *she'd* been wearing a costume ever since her mother had left, and she had been looking forward to taking it off just for one night.

Instead she was stuck tracking down her dad and

hoping he'd had enough sense to finally show up for his shift tonight. A text from Ethan had come in just as Audrey was exiting the carousel and heading over to buy Grace's funnel cake:

Dad still isn't here. Are you sure he's coming?

No, Audrey had texted back. But I'll find him.

The carnival was getting busier, and the lines were getting longer. She pushed through the crowd and hurried over to the front of the Ferris wheel. "Hey, no cuts!" yelled a small boy hidden behind a cloud of cotton candy. To Audrey's great relief she saw her father, clean-shaven and neatly dressed in a polo shirt and cargo pants. He had one hand on the ride controls; the other grasped a steel coffee thermos.

"Dad? You all right?"

"Just dandy," he said, taking a swig from the thermos. "Why?"

"Um . . . just wondering. How's work going tonight?"

He snorted. "The carnies are morons. Have sticks shoved up their you-know-whats."

"Why?" Audrey asked carefully. "Did something happen?"

"They thought I was late, but I was actually early. When I got here the lights at the Snack Emporium weren't hung correctly—half the carnies here don't have the first clue what they're doing—so I thought I'd pitch in and help out before someone got hurt, especially since Russ had investors coming in tonight, or so everyone is saying. Then I had to help shut down the Fishing for Fortune ride, because a bunch of the boats broke. Then I got chewed out for not being *here*, at the Ferris wheel, on time—even though I told one of them where I was and what I was doing."

Just then a burst of static crackled from the walkie-talkie hooked to his belt: *"Maintenance, do you copy? We need to get someone down to the Clown Faces ASAP. The ride is jammed."*

"See what I mean?" he growled. "Morons, all of them—these people's idea of safety is a joke."

"So . . . you're sure you were here on time?" she pressed.

"Audrey—what did I just say?"

At his exasperated look, she said, "I know, but someone told Ethan you showed up late."

He scowled. "Some people in this town just want to believe the worst about me."

Audrey averted her eyes. She didn't want to be counted among those who doubted him, but it was kind of hard when he kept such erratic hours. Most nights she had absolutely no idea where he was or what he was doing. Sure, he said he was working. But where? And what about those strange phone calls he sometimes got late at night when he thought Audrey was asleep?

"Didn't you tell me that besides the free tickets you got a couple of free coupons for the Snack Emporium?" Audrey asked, deciding to change the subject. "Do you have one for a funnel cake?"

He shook his head. "I only had a couple for chili fries, which I gave to Ethan. Why?"

"Well . . . I sort of need to buy someone a funnel cake."

He frowned. "Why do you need to do that?"

Now Audrey shook her head; she had no idea how to explain the inner workings of Julia King's brain. "I just need to get one, and I don't have any money. . . . It's for Grace Chang."

She wished he would say, "We don't have money to spend ten bucks on one tiny funnel cake. We need to save." But there was no way he'd say no, not to Grace Chang.

Because the truth was, on the night the Carlson Factory burned down, one man died. But *two* men were hospitalized: Grace's dad and Audrey's dad. Mr. McKinley had been working late that night in the factory. He'd been sleeping there, actually, when the fire started. By the time the fire department arrived, nothing could be done to save the structure. But Mr. Chang had recognized his best friend's beat-up Chevy parked out front. He'd plunged inside and found Audrey's father sprawled on the couch in his office, seemingly unconscious from smoke inhalation. He picked him up and dragged him through the burning building. He'd collapsed just as he'd reached the door to the outside.

Mr. Chang was the hero who gave his life for his best friend. But every good story needs both a hero and a villain. As word spread about the fire, Mr. McKinley quickly became that villain. He was the good-for-nothing husband who should have been home with his brood of kids and depressed wife. Instead he was sleeping at the factory, and because of him, Henry "Home Run" Chang wouldn't be coming home to *his* family ever again.

"Here," Mr. McKinley said now, digging furiously through his pockets. "Here's ten for the funnel cake. And here's another twenty for anything else she needs."

"Dad, we don't have the—"

"You give that poor girl anything she wants tonight," he interrupted, a ragged edge in his voice. "You hear me, Audrey? Anything." Just hearing Grace's name seemed to age him, and Audrey thought maybe it was better that Grace and her mother were moving away. She felt bad for thinking it—Grace had been one of the best friends she'd ever had—but Mrs. Chang had made it clear she didn't want to have anything to do with the down-on-their-luck McKinleys.

Except before the fire, Mr. McKinley hadn't been down on his luck, not really. He'd had a good job as the manager of the Carlson Factory. He had a big family that he loved. Sure, he and Audrey's mom fought occasionally. Well, more than occasionally—enough that he often stayed late at work and slept in his office at the factory. But overall, life was good.

Until the fire changed everything and Grace lost her father, who had been trying to save both Mr. Carlson's factory and Mr. McKinley's life.

Afterward, Mrs. Chang said she didn't want her or Grace to have anything to do with the McKinleys or the Carlsons anymore—it was just too painful. Mr. McKinley and Mr. Carlson were both wracked with grief, and whenever they saw each other it just reminded them of the friend they'd lost. It got so bad the two men couldn't stand to be in the same room together.

And all that was why Audrey, Harlow, and Grace—

who had been best friends since the time they could walk—didn't speak to each other anymore.

The line for funnel cakes had grown much longer. Audrey figured she'd have to miss a couple rides, then catch up with Julia and the others.

Where are you guys? she texted Julia. I'm getting Grace's funnel cake.

She waited, but when Julia didn't text back right away Audrey occupied herself by looking up her friends' online accounts. Her stomach dropped when she saw a picture Erin had posted. It was a photo of Harlow—a really terrible one. Not only did it seem like Harlow was about to pick her nose, but her eyes were glazed over and it looked like she was drooling.

Audrey wanted to vomit. It was a cruel picture, and as she stared a couple comments came in:

she's so gross

She looks like a zombie!

Without even thinking about it, her fingers engaged in their usual dance, tapping and swiping until she was one click away from reposting the picture. She reposted pictures all the time and never thought anything of it; with every new post she always hoped she'd get more likes or followers. It wasn't until her thumb was poised to hit send that her mind finally caught up with her fingers. What was she thinking? *Of course* she couldn't repost a nasty picture of Harlow. She wouldn't . . . Even though she knew if she *did* she'd probably get her three hundredth follower. Her thumb continued hovering over the screen until she finally let out a breath and stuck her phone back in her pocket.

Maybe, just for a little bit, she'd stay offline.

A minute later she was already bored. What did she do to kill time before she had a phone? The line stretched long before her, and she was tempted to leave and tell Julia she wasn't her personal errand girl. Except she really did want Grace to have a funnel cake. At least she could take off her pipe-cleaner tiara for a few minutes since Julia wasn't around; the thing had been digging into her scalp all night.

At that moment, she glanced over and happened to

17

Grace

"YOU SHOULDN'T HAVE POSTED THAT PICTURE," Grace said to Erin as they passed the Zipper, a ride with cages that spun upside down.

Grace hated the Zipper. And nasty pictures that people should have known not to post online.

Erin didn't appear to have heard her. She was walking next to Julia, laughing as she showed her the comments lighting up her phone. Grace walked silently behind them while Lulu also checked her phone.

After Ethan threw up, everyone quickly exited the

ride and the girls parted company with the boys. Jean had said she'd needed to go check in with her parents. Since then, no one had been able to decide which ride to go on next; everyone was too busy checking their phones to talk about it.

"You shouldn't have posted it," Grace repeated, but no one paid any attention to her. She knew she should have pushed the point further. But she couldn't bring herself to speak again. Sometimes she felt like the loudest person in the universe. But the loudness was only in her own head. In reality, she was the quietest girl in school.

But lately—ever since she found out she was moving—she'd had dreams that when she got to California she'd arrive a completely different person. Someone who wasn't afraid to speak all the thoughts swirling inside her.

Once Julia had enough of looking at the picture, she announced, "Let's go find Diego."

"Okay," Grace mumbled. She felt so awful about the picture of Harlow she couldn't bring herself to care about Julia's crush on Diego or the destroyed pumpkin gram.

Last week she'd overheard something in the library she was pretty sure she wasn't supposed to hear. Julia and Erin had been huddled together at a table, their math homework forgotten while they whispered and giggled. Grace hadn't meant to eavesdrop, but she was right behind them, looking for a book about California. Their voices carried and she could only hear snatches of the conversation. But the moment Julia uttered the words "Harlow" and "prank" and "carnival," Grace's ears had pricked up. She'd thought she'd also overheard the word "midnight," but she was less sure about that.

Grace had leaned closer; she'd almost knocked the bookshelf over, but she hadn't been able to hear exactly what prank they'd been planning to play on Harlow. She had been so worried earlier tonight as she walked to the carnival. But since she hadn't seen Harlow all night, she'd relaxed and figured it didn't matter: You can't play a prank on someone who isn't there.

Except Grace had forgotten how the online world

could reach right into the real world and mess everything up.

"You shouldn't have posted it," Grace said yet again,
but Julia, Erin, and Lulu continued to ignore her. That
was typical. They rarely paid attention to what Grace
actually said—when she bothered to speak at all. Julia
sometimes treated Grace like she was some sort of
celebrity. But Grace had a feeling that if her dad had
survived the fire, things would be different. Right after
the fire Grace had been in a fog, and it had felt good not
to make any decisions, to just sit quietly at their usual
lunch table and let everyone else's words wash over her
like soothing white noise. Lately, though, that fog was
lifting and things were becoming clear.

Julia and Erin had changed a lot since Mrs. Bronson's
fourth-grade class. Back then, Julia and Erin had loved
bubble gum more than boys. They'd have contests to see
who could blow the biggest bubble—then pop them with
their hands. Neither of them had ever cared when the
gum got stuck in their braids—and they never would have
posted a picture like that of Harlow online.

What was happening to everyone? Sometimes Grace felt like she didn't recognize her friends anymore. Then again, there were days when she didn't recognize herself, either.

Grace realized she didn't much like Erin and Julia anymore. But it wasn't like she was planning on *saying* that to them; they were just thoughts she would leave behind in Clarkville.

But even if she couldn't speak some of the thoughts inside her head, that didn't mean she couldn't text them.

She pulled out her phone and hunted for Harlow's number.

18

Harlow

HARLOW USED TO BE SCARED OF MONSTERS, the kind with pointy teeth and sharp claws that stalk little kids in the middle of the night. When she was younger, she envisioned them everywhere. In her closet. In the attic. Underneath her bed. But one night when she was feeling brave, she threw open her closet door and discovered it was empty, and that the monsters weren't real.

Now Harlow feared monsters of a different sort. The kind that could be unleashed by a cruel photo. The kind that could keep multiplying with every awful comment posted online.

Comments that, so far, she hadn't read.

Because unfortunately, these kinds of monsters *were* real, and Harlow wasn't in any rush to confront them. And yet, at the same time she felt a curious, almost electric pull toward her phone, and she had to keep telling herself not to look at what everyone might be saying about her online. That it was better not to know.

After Ethan had thrown up, she'd excused herself, telling everyone she needed to find her parents, and that she'd see them all later. She'd fled to the vendor area and headed straight for the city government booth where her mother was chatting with council members. Once inside she took off her costume. Her father had entered a minute later with the mayor and the investors from Boston.

"Harlow!" her dad had said. "I'm so glad you came. Gentlemen, ladies—this is my daughter, Harlow."

"Pleased to meet you," Harlow said to them, shaking hands with each one.

"How do you like living in Clarkville?" one of them asked her. Behind him, Mr. Carlson stared at her expectantly. He had a hopeful smile on his face and deep circles under his eyes. Harlow knew he stayed up most nights worrying about Clarkville's future. Her father would never ride the carousel—or any carnival ride, for that matter—but if he did and he'd made some wishes, every single one of them would have been about rebuilding the factory.

"Clarkville is the best city in the world," she answered. Then she excused herself and slunk to the back of the booth, where she took out her phone and slid to the ground.

She'd been holding her phone in her hands, staring at the picture for several minutes now, telling herself not to look at the comments. Curiosity was burning a hole in her heart, though, and finally she gave up and scrolled downward. Things were even worse than she'd imagined:

she's so gross

She looks like a zombie!

Disgusting!

Harlow Carlson makes me sick

I hope she dyes

idiot its dies not dyes

youre the idiot

She's a giant!

She's as tall as King Kong.

lol and just as hairy too

zombie girl

nosepicker

Harlow Carlson has a mustache!

That last one hurt worse than the others. Harlow—like a lot of the Carlsons on her dad's side—had ruddy skin and dark, wiry hair. And okay, yeah, sometimes her upper lip *was* a little shadowy lately, but so what? Why did that have to mean she was gross or disgusting? Why did other people get to decide that about her?

Harlow touched the top of her upper lip and fought back tears. On and on the comments came, each one pulling her heart a little lower. The picture was everywhere; kids were reposting it on their own accounts. A couple of her classmates had texted the picture directly to her, just to make sure she knew how much everyone hated her.

Her phone buzzed with a text. It was from Grace:

Grace: Thought you should know there's a nasty picture of you going around. May want to stay offline.

Harlow: Too late. I've seen it.

Grace: I'm so sorry.

Harlow: It's okay.

It wasn't okay, not by a long shot, but this was the longest conversation they'd had in nearly a year, and Harlow didn't want it to end.

Harlow: I heard you're moving tomorrow.

Grace: Yeah. To stupid California. Are you at the carnival?

Harlow paused before answering. She didn't want to lie to Grace, but she also didn't want to tell her that "Jean" was really Harlow, so she decided to ignore the question.

Harlow: Really mad about the picture. I'm going to text Erin.

Grace: That's a bad idea.

Harlow: I don't care. I'll text you later.

Harlow punched in Erin's number, and for good measure, Julia's, and started a text thread:

Harlow: Erin I saw the picture. That was low.

Erin: Can't you take a joke?

Julia: I thought your hair looked pretty.

Erin: Yeah, I liked your hair too. I didn't even realize how the rest of the picture looked until after I posted it.

Julia: You really do have great hair.

Harlow felt confused; did they really mean those nice things about her hair? She pulled up the picture again and . . . actually, her hair *did* look kind of good. But she'd been on the Clown Faces with them; she *knew* they'd realized it was a bad picture. That's why Grace had tried to stop Erin from posting it.

Harlow wanted to scream in frustration. She knew she should put her phone away. But texting with her old friends was giving her a secret thrill. Also, for so long she'd felt like a person who'd been left to starve on a desert island, and these compliments from Julia and

Erin were like finding a sugary cake and a cold, sparkling soda—even if she knew she shouldn't trust them.

"Harlow? Are you still in here?" came her mother's voice.

"Back here," Harlow answered. She put down her phone. She'd finish texting everyone later.

"I'm so glad you came!" Mrs. Carlson said. "So far everything seems to be going well. Everyone liked eating at Frank's, and the gift baskets were a hit, and—" Upon seeing the crushed look on Harlow's face, she paused. "What's wrong?"

"Nothing. Just . . . a couple kids at school posted a nasty picture of me on the Internet."

Mrs. Carlson's eyes narrowed. "What do you mean?" she said sharply. "What kind of picture?"

"I was looking out the window at school and—"

"Wait, in one of your classes?" she sounded relieved. "No one spied on you?"

"Well, no. I guess not," Harlow said.

How could she explain that it felt like someone *had* been spying on her? That she'd been caught in a moment, lost in thought over the mysterious pumpkin gram, and someone had decided to capture that moment and broadcast it to the entire school. And just as bad, they—Erin—had waited until she was sitting at an awkward angle to take the picture.

"I want to see it," Mrs. Carlson said.

"Um . . . okay." Harlow obeyed, but she enlarged the photo so it took up the entire screen. No way was she going to let her mother see the comments.

"Wow . . . ," Mrs. Carlson said, seeming to search for the right words. "Well . . . that's just . . ."

"Awful," Harlow supplied. "It's okay. You can say it— it's awful."

"Well . . . yes," Mrs. Carlson said finally. "It really is." Harlow cracked a small grin, and Mrs. Carlson said, "What are you going to do now?"

"Ignore it as best I can." *And hide in here the rest of the night*, she added to herself.

Mrs. Carlson scowled as she continued looking at the picture. "Erin Donoghue posted it? I'm going to say something to her mother." She began tapping at her own phone and Harlow quickly covered the screen with her hand.

"No!" Harlow said quickly. "That will just make things worse."

"But—"

"Mom—seriously, don't text Mrs. Donoghue. Promise me, okay?"

Mrs. Carlson sighed and put her phone away. "I promise," she said, but she didn't look happy about it.

"Good," Harlow replied. "You don't happen to have your laptop with you, do you?" she added quickly, hoping to change the subject. She did *not* want her mother contacting Mrs. Donoghue; that would be even tougher to live down than the photo itself.

"I think I left it in my car. Why?"

Briefly Harlow explained her project. "I thought maybe I could present it to the investors tomorrow. Give them something visual to see how special Clarkville is." She pulled up some of the photos she'd already taken. "See? I've got some great shots of the town, and the carnival, and I've started interviewing people. I just need a laptop to start putting everything together."

"These are great photos," Mrs. Carlson said. When she looked back up, her eyes were shining with something that Harlow suspected might be pride. "This is a great idea—I'm going to go tell your dad about it!"

Just as her mother headed for the front of the tent, Harlow's phone buzzed with more texts:

Erin: Where R U? We're about to ride the Zipper.

Julia: Are you at the carnival?

Harlow thought long and hard before texting back:

No, I stayed home tonight.

A few minutes later, Mrs. Carlson returned, a bright smile lighting up her face. "Your dad thinks it's an excellent idea! He'd actually like you to close the meeting with your presentation. I'll go get my laptop right now." Just before she left, she turned back and said, "That may not be a great photo of you, but you're a great kid, and a beautiful girl—you know that, right?"

"Sure," Harlow said, although she didn't know that. Not really. Most days she felt strange and awkward and like she didn't quite fit into her own body. She secretly dreamed sometimes that one day she'd wake up—like a princess from a long, deep sleep—and suddenly feel confident and beautiful and wonderful, all at the same time. She'd thought about wishing for it on the carousel but decided against it.

Some wishes, she knew, took their own sweet time to come true.

19

Audrey

AUDREY GOT OUT OF THE LINE FOR FUNNEL cakes and followed the woman in the pirate costume. She never got a look at her face, but she thought she saw a tendril of curly red hair—the exact same shade as her mother's—pull free from the woman's pirate hat.

Could her mother be *here*? In Clarkville and at the carnival? Audrey guessed it was possible; her mother had loved the carnival—it had been her favorite night of the whole year.

She swallowed; but if her mother was back in town,

why hadn't she come home? Didn't she know how much Audrey needed her?

She followed the woman, pushing her way through the thick crowd, until all at once Audrey couldn't see her anymore. She came to a stop and heard screaming overhead.

She looked up; the cages of the Zipper were spinning just above her, and she could swear she saw the gleeful faces of Erin and Julia inside as they came bearing down upon her. Audrey ducked, certain she was going to be crushed. Then the cages were snatched away and went spinning back upward into the air.

"Watch where you're going!" the carnie operating the Zipper yelled. "Stay behind the yellow line."

"Sorry," Audrey mumbled. She stepped away and glanced over just in time to see the woman in the pirate costume duck into an extremely large, red-velvet tent. Audrey hurried over, but just as she was about to enter, a voice said, "Hold it right there." A carnie with a bald head and a row of eyebrow rings blocked her way.

"I need to get inside," Audrey said, trying to move past him, but he wouldn't budge.

"Sorry, no can do."

"But that woman just walked right in."

"*She* works here. You have to have one of these, see?" He flashed a staff badge that had his name and position. He was Stan Axelrod and he was doing security.

Audrey stared at the tent. Could it be that her mother was working for the carnival? She had always been intrigued by the carnies and said it must have been exciting to wake up every weekend in a new city. But when she said it, Audrey figured it was just another one of her spells she was going through, where she'd lie in bed for hours and dream of the other lives she'd rather have than the one she did have: being a wife and a mother in Clarkville.

Had she done it? Had her mother become a carnie?

Audrey spent the next twenty minutes standing by the tent, waiting for the woman to come back outside. But the only thing that happened was that Stan the Security Man just stood there glaring at her.

Ethan passed by with a few of his friends.

"Hey, Audrey!" called Travis McManus. "Your brother puked on the Clown Faces."

"Shut up," Ethan said. "Why do you always have to be such a—"

"I saw Mom," Audrey blurted.

Ethan froze. "What?"

"I saw Mom," she said again. "She's *here*."

Ethan let out an irritated breath, then turned to his friends. "I'll catch up to you guys later," he said. After they'd left, he turned back to Audrey and said, "You didn't see Mom."

"Yes, I did. She's inside that tent." She pointed and Stan Axelrod glared at her some more.

"Audrey—Mom split. She's not coming back, okay? Can't you understand that? She didn't love us, so she left."

"That's not true." Audrey shook her head. "She did love us. She *does*."

"Then where is she?" he spread his hands wide. "Nowhere, that's where. She's left us with *him*." She knew Ethan was angry at their dad, but the hatred in his voice made her take a step back.

She wished everyone knew certain things about

Ethan—like how he used to make sure their mother took her medication every day so she wouldn't get too sad. That he secretly liked to write poetry and got good grades in English. That he was really sad when Audrey stopped hanging out with Grace and Harlow. But right now he looked exactly like the troublemaker some people in town thought he was.

"I saw her," Audrey insisted. "I don't care if you believe me or not." She glanced at the tent and lowered her voice. "Listen, if you wanted to get inside that tent but it was for staff only, how would you do it?"

He shrugged. "Pretend to be staff," he said. "But you won't find Mom in there because she's *not here*, Audrey."

"But—"

She was interrupted when her phone buzzed with an alert. Someone else had reposted the awful picture of Harlow.

"Have you seen this?" she said, showing her phone to Ethan, who made a face.

"Yeah," he said. "I've seen it."

"Some of your friends have posted really nasty comments about her."

"So what?" he said, sounding defensive. "It was *your* friend who posted the picture in the first place."

"Can't you make everyone stop?" Audrey asked.

"What do you want *me* to do?"

"Tell them to stop."

Ethan rolled his eyes. But he pulled out his phone and posted: All right you guys. This is getting stupid. Leave Harlow alone.

But his words only set off another round of comments:

Do you LIKE Harlow?

dude i didn't know you liked hairy women

Aww Ethan luvs Harlow

Ethan and Harlow sitting in a tree . . .

On and on the comments poured in, some so nasty Audrey would have gotten in trouble if she'd repeated the words.

"I can't look at this anymore," Ethan said finally. "You just can't win with this stuff."

No, Audrey thought sadly. *You really can't.*

20

Grace

SO FAR AT LEAST ONE OF GRACE'S CAROUSEL wishes was coming true: She hadn't received any irate texts from her mother telling her to come home, which meant she was still out with her book club friends. Was it too much to hope she'd stay out really late so Grace could make it to the Ferris wheel? Grace had been trying not to think too much about the pumpkin gram stuffed in her pocket, but now she was starting to wonder: When she went to the Ferris wheel, who would be waiting for her?

"Let's go on the Fun Slide again," Erin was saying.

"The Fun Slide always hurts my butt," Lulu said.

Grace was quietly listening to everyone argue about what to do next while she checked her phone. They still hadn't been able to find Diego—a huge relief to Grace—so they'd ended up riding on the Zipper instead. Grace was hoping Julia had forgotten all about him.

Her phone lit up with another comment on Harlow's picture, but Grace wasn't as worried now. Harlow had texted Julia and Erin and said that she wasn't coming to the carnival—and even though Grace had secretly really wanted to see her tonight, she figured it was probably best now if Harlow stayed home.

A text came in then. It was from Diego:

I have something important to tell you. Are you at the carnival?

"No, I don't want to ride the Ferris wheel," Julia was saying.

"Why not?" Lulu said. "That's your favorite ride. You said so yesterday."

Grace's heart pounded wildly as she stared at Diego's text. Was another one of her carousel wishes coming true? And what important thing did he have to tell her?

Yes. I'm here, she texted back.

His response was immediate: Can we meet?

Before Grace could reply, Lulu suddenly leaned over and shouted, "Julia, ohmigosh! Diego just texted Grace!"

Julia whirled around. "What did he say?" she demanded.

"He says he has something important to tell her," Lulu answered. "And he wants to meet her somewhere!"

"Let me see." Julia held her palm out, and Grace felt she had no choice but to hand over her phone.

Julia took it and began tapping at the screen. "What are you doing?" Grace said.

"I'm coming up with a plan," Julia answered.

Grace swallowed. "What did you text him?"

"See for yourself." She turned Grace's phone around so they could all read her message:

Yes. Meet me at the kissing booth.

Grace wanted to die, right then and there. Was this her wish, coming true? Or was it all spinning away from her, blowing away like dandelion fluff?

"Wait," said Lulu. "I don't get it. Won't he think Grace wants to kiss him?"

"Be serious," Julia snapped. "*Of course* he doesn't think Grace wants to kiss him."

Why not? Grace said, only to herself.

"What's the plan, then?" Erin said.

Julia beckoned everyone closer. "Come here," she said.

They huddled up like a football team; the music, the laughter, and the lights of the carnival whirling all around them. Julia was their quarterback, calling the play. And the play was this: Grace would meet Diego at the Kissing Booth and hear what he had to say. The rest of them would hang back a bit. Julia had no doubt that the important thing Diego wanted to discuss with Grace was Julia herself, and the pumpkin gram she'd sent him. Grace was to listen to him and then call for Julia, who would seemingly appear out of thin air.

"Like a vision," Erin said in a breathy voice.

Or a ghoul, Grace said, but only to herself. Out loud, she said, "Then what do I do?"

"Then you can leave us alone," Julia said.

"Gee, thanks," Grace said, this time to everyone, but she said it so softly that no one heard.

They broke out of the huddle and made their way to the Kissing Booth, passing monsters and mimes and puppeteers and stilt walkers. Grace felt the night was taking on a grotesque tone. She had wished to kiss Diego at the carnival, and now she was headed to meet him at the Kissing Booth—so *Julia* could see him. Things felt inside out and upside down and all kinds of weird.

And most important of all: Would Diego and Julia actually kiss?

It seemed Julia hoped they would. As they walked she fluffed her hair and whispered to Erin, "Get a good picture—right as our lips lock. Take a bunch, too. I don't want to post one where I look gross," she said, which made Grace so mad her fingernails bit her palms.

Did Julia even *like* Diego? Or did she just want

another selfie she could post? Grace knew Julia and Audrey were quietly competing for likes and followers online—maybe Julia figured a kissing picture would put her over the top?

Grace kicked at a stray popcorn kernel. This was turning out to be a rotten night.

The Kissing Booth—a red-and-white-striped wooden stand—came into view, and Diego was standing right in front, waiting. The lights from the carnival shone down on him and his black hair was slicked into shiny spikes.

"There he is!" Lulu squealed.

"He's so cute!" Erin said.

"Be cool, everyone," Julia said. She turned to Grace. "We'll hang back here," she said, gesturing to a stand that sold caramel apples. "When it's time, give me the signal and then I'll come over."

"Okay," Grace said, and started forward. As she walked toward him, for one small second she allowed herself to believe that her wish was coming true. That Diego liked her and wanted to tell her so, and that it had been *his* idea to meet at the Kissing Booth.

Why *did* he want to meet her, anyway? It obviously had nothing to do with Julia or with the pumpkin gram he'd never received. What did he want to tell her?

"Hi, Grace," he said as she drew near. He frowned. "What's that you're wearing?" He pointed at her red feather boa.

She shrugged. "Just some stupid costume Julia made us all wear—I've also got a tiara under my baseball cap."

"Oh," Diego said. "Cool." He looked nervous; his Adam's apple was bobbing up and down furiously. He shoved his hands into his coat pockets and leaned close. "I have something to tell you," he whispered.

Was he really going to kiss her, right then and there? A part of her wanted him to, but a part of her felt like she was trapped in a horror show. What would happen if he kissed her in front of Julia? She'd be on Julia's bad side for sure.

But honestly . . . how much did Grace need to care, since next week she'd be starting a new school, far away from Clarkville and its darkening autumn? When she'd be in California, where the sun always shone?

Not much, Grace decided. In fact, she decided she didn't care at all. Not if it meant she could get her first kiss and her own magical carnival story.

"What is it?" She leaned forward and her eyes fluttered shut. She couldn't help it. She'd imagined this moment a million times.

Bright spots shaped like shiny red lips danced on the back of her eyelids. She heard Diego take a deep breath and sensed him lean in even closer. Felt his warm breath on her cheeks as he whispered, "Our parents are dating."

21

Audrey

3 HOURS TO MIDNIGHT

AUDREY WAS WALKING THROUGH THE carnival, trying to find Julia and the others. After she'd left Ethan, it had taken her at least half an hour to finally get through the funnel cake line. When she got to the front, she realized she had no idea what flavor Grace wanted. She finally picked out salted caramel butterscotch, hoping it was the right one. The carnie making it had given her an extremely small and extremely overcooked one, then sighed deeply when Audrey asked him to box it up to go. Then she'd looped around the carnival trying to find everyone. She'd also texted Julia—again—asking where they were, but so far Julia hadn't texted her back.

She'd been trying to forget about the woman in the pirate costume. Ethan was right; it couldn't be their mother. Wherever their mother was, she wasn't here, wearing a costume and pretending to be a carnie.

But still . . .

After she'd made another loop and still hadn't found her friends, she decided to go back to the velvet tent. Stan Axelrod had left; in his place was another man, someone she hadn't ever seen before. She decided to try one last time to get inside.

She approached the man and said, "My mother is in there—can I get in? There's something I'd like to give her."

Actually, there were several things she'd love to give her mother the next time she saw her: A hug, a kiss, and a lecture about a mile long that could be summed up in one sentence: "How could you have just *left* us?"

"She need something for the show?" the man asked, his eyes straying to the box Audrey was carrying.

"Uh, yeah," Audrey answered quickly, although she had no idea what he was talking about. She opened up the box and showed him the overcooked piece of dough. "She asked for this funnel cake."

"That's not a funnel cake," he answered, shaking his head as he opened the door to the tent. "That there's a deep-fried disappointment."

Audrey shrugged and stepped inside with her deep-fried disappointment. The door closed behind her, plunging her into darkness. She blinked rapidly until her eyes adjusted, then followed a silver slice of light down a long hall until she came to a crowded room.

It was a dressing room of sorts. Rows of costumes piped the edges of the room like colorful frosting. Mirrored tables sat in the middle where men and women were touching up their makeup. Some were dressed as mimes, some as clowns, some as acrobats.

"Are you from the Snack Emporium?" a girl wearing a white-and-black-striped leotard asked. "I think you've got my lucky funnel cake." She held her hands out and

Audrey reluctantly handed it over. Great, now she'd have to stand in line a *third* time.

"Wait." The girl looked up quizzically. "I thought I ordered red velvet?"

"Uh, you did," Audrey replied quickly. "But we were out, so I brought you this one instead."

"But—"

"Oh, hurry up and eat it, Glenda," called a woman dressed as a mermaid. "We go on in fifteen."

"We go on after I've eaten my lucky funnel cake," Glenda retorted. "It's tradition." She took a bite, powdered sugar working its way around the edges of her mouth as she chewed. When she caught sight of Audrey still staring at her, she said, "Something wrong?"

Audrey took a deep breath. "I'm looking for my mother. I think she's in here somewhere."

"Oh yeah? What's her name?"

"Tricia." Her mother's name tasted strange on Audrey's tongue. She was having trouble getting the words out. "Tricia Mc—"

"I know who Tricia is," Glenda said. "She's over by the lips."

Audrey frowned. "The lips?"

Glenda pointed a greasy finger. "That way."

Audrey moved on and soon saw Glenda wasn't kidding. A large pair of neon-colored purple lips framed a black door. Hidden to the side, steeped in the shadows, was a woman. Audrey's heart began hammering. Could it really be her mother?

But as she drew near, she quickly realized it was not. This woman looked nothing at all like her mother. She was wearing a baby doll costume and had blond hair and a bulky frame. She was definitely not the woman Audrey had followed earlier that night.

"You need something, kid?"

"Uh, no. I—just—you're not Tricia McKinley," Audrey said.

"No kidding," the woman replied. "I'm Tricia Rhodes. Is there a problem?"

"Oh, no," Audrey said. "I just—I thought you might be my mother."

Sometimes disappointment doesn't taste deep-fried. Sometimes it's fresh and so raw it squirms in your throat and won't go away, no matter how many times you try to swallow it down.

"Why would you think I was your mother?" Tricia Rhodes asked, and Audrey shrugged. "What's your name?" Tricia added.

"Audrey."

"Okay, *Audrey*. You look a bit young. Do you work here?"

"I delivered a funnel cake—but I was just leaving," she added quickly, because she had no idea how much trouble she'd be in if anyone realized she'd lied her way into the place.

The overhead lights began to flash and a voice called out, *"Ten minutes, everyone!"*

A carnie with yellowing teeth came striding up to Tricia. "Twyla called in sick tonight with a migraine, which means we're down a twirler. We need someone to go into the Belly of the Beast with Lynn."

Twirler? Belly of the Beast? The conversation

seemed nonsensical to Audrey, and with the lights flashing she was having trouble seeing anything but blinking shadows.

The carnie caught sight of Audrey then and said, "Who are you?"

"She's a delivery girl," Tricia answered. "And she was just leaving. Right?"

"Right," Audrey answered.

"Lynn can just go on by herself tonight," Tricia said, and both she and the carnie left. They seemed to have already forgotten about Audrey.

Audrey meant to leave, she really did, but right then she wondered: Was there a stage on the other side of the door?

Audrey loved stages. Any type of stage—even virtual ones like her social media accounts where she posted images and videos, or the small, literal one inside her school's multipurpose room where she'd had the lead in the school play last year. She would die if anyone knew this, but she oftentimes dreamed of becoming a famous actress—the kind that won shiny awards and made long speeches thanking all the people who helped them along the way.

A girl dressed in black pants and a black tank top appeared, carrying two black batons.

"Oh, *twirling*!" Audrey said, happy that things were finally starting to make sense. "Baton twirling—*that's* what they meant!"

"Uh, yeah," the girl said, staring at her strangely. "Are you Twyla's replacement?"

The loudspeakers crackled to life and a voice boomed, *"Ladies and gentlemen, welcome to the Belly of the Beast!"*

The girl quickly pressed a baton into Audrey's hand. "That's our cue," she said. She tapped a button on her baton and sparks shot out either end. "See you out there," she called as she opened the door and stepped onstage.

Through the open door Audrey heard music and thunderous applause, and caught a glimpse of what appeared to be a thousand pinpricks of light that could easily be mistaken for stars. But they weren't stars.

Members of the audience had their phones up, waiting to record the show.

Audrey wondered if her mother was somewhere out there in the dark. She had to be *somewhere*, didn't she? What if she was watching the show right now?

Audrey didn't have to think twice. She pressed the button, her baton ignited, and she stepped onstage.

▶ 22 ◀

Grace

"WHAT?" GRACE BLINKED. NO WAY DID SHE hear that right.

"Our parents are dating," Diego repeated. "I had a feeling you didn't know. They're actually on a date right now."

"That can't be true." Grace shook her head. Her mother was spending the night with her boring book club. She'd said so herself.

But, Grace suddenly remembered, she'd also spent a ton of time picking out her dress for tonight, something that now struck Grace as pretty odd.

"Are you okay?" Diego asked. "You don't look so good."

"I'm just hungry," Grace said. "I never ate dinner." Her stomach chose that moment to let out a very embarrassing gurgling sound, one that would make you think of trips to the bathroom, not kisses at the carnival.

"Want to split some popcorn?" Diego said, pointing to the snack stand next to the Kissing Booth.

"Sure," Grace answered, feeling dazed. She guessed if she couldn't share a kiss with Diego, she'd settle for sharing popcorn.

While Diego paid for the popcorn, Grace checked her phone, which had been pinging with increasingly impatient texts from Julia:

Why is this taking so long?

What are you two doing?

WHAT IS GOING ON?!?!!??

Just give me a minute, Grace texted back.

After Diego finished paying he handed Grace the bag of popcorn, and she began eating hungrily. "So, do you believe me?" he asked.

"I don't know what to think," Grace said.

Diego suddenly glanced over her shoulder. "Follow me," he said, and began walking away. "Before we lose them."

"What did you say?" Grace sprinted to catch up with him, but he didn't answer her. Her phone pinged with another text from Julia:

WHERE ARE YOU GOING?

Grace looked backward; Julia and the rest of them were following her and Diego. That girl Jean must have caught up to them while Grace was talking to Diego, because she was right next to Julia, who had a murderous look on her face.

"In here," Diego said. He ushered her into a large velvet circus tent. Inside was a circular stage, ringed with rows of wooden seating. A brass sign above the stage said **WELCOME TO THE BELLY OF THE BEAST!**

Diego led them to a couple seats near the back. Grace could hear the row behind her filling and felt a sharp poke in the back.

"What's going on?" came Julia's fierce whisper in her ear. "Why are we here?"

Diego, who had been busy scanning the room, suddenly said, "Look two rows up and to the left."

Grace looked; exactly two rows up and to the left her mother and Mr. Martinez were taking seats next to each other. Mr. Martinez held a bag of popcorn, which he offered to Grace's mother.

"See," Diego said. "I told you. They came here together tonight. On a *date*," he added.

Grace could only nod mutely. Mr. Martinez was a firefighter, like her dad had been, and one Saturday morning a few years ago they held a baseball game against Fairvale's fire department. The Clarkville station nearly lost because Mr. Martinez was an awful pitcher.

Grace didn't want to think about her mother seeing anyone. But she felt very strongly that if her mother ever *did* start dating again, she should at least choose someone who could throw a decent fastball.

Decent pitching skills or not, here they were at the carnival. Together. Which meant her mother had *lied*. Not only was she not meeting with her book club, she was on a date. So much for Team Chang. *How long have they been dating?* Grace wondered. *And how serious are they?*

If her mother and Mr. Martinez got married, that would make Grace and Diego family. Then Grace would be in the unfortunate position of being in love with her stepbrother, which was just totally disgusting.

"I had a feeling no one told you," Diego said.

"Is it serious?" Grace asked.

"Well," Diego said slowly, "my dad is talking about visiting California next summer."

The lights flashed overhead and a voice from the loudspeakers boomed, *"Ladies and gentlemen, welcome to the Belly of the Beast!"* Music began to play, and the audience burst into applause. Just then, right before the lights faded, Grace's mother looked over and their eyes met. Even from across the room Grace could see her swelling with fury.

Her mother stood up.

Grace also stood up. Then she grabbed Diego's hand and said, "Run!"

Harlow

"*NOW WHERE ARE THEY GOING?*" JULIA SAID as Grace and Diego sprinted away.

"They're running from Grace's mom," Lulu said. "Look."

They all looked; Mrs. Chang was storming up the aisle just as the curtain lifted and two baton twirlers burst onto the stage.

"Uh-oh, busted," Erin said. She turned to Harlow. "Grace sneaked out of the house tonight. She wasn't supposed to go to the carnival."

From behind her mask Harlow nodded as she blindly watched the show. She had meant to stay in the tent the rest of the night and work on her presentation, she really had. But after interviewing each member of the city council, she decided she wanted a snack. With that awful picture of her floating around, there was no way she was going back to the carnival without her costume. She figured it would just be a quick trip to the Snack Emporium and back. She hadn't counted on running into everyone while they waited for Grace and Diego to finish talking at the Kissing Booth.

As soon as Erin had called "Jean!," Harlow had been tempted to rip off her mask and start yelling at her. But Erin had immediately started talking about Julia's big plan to get a selfie with Diego at the Kissing Booth. She'd been so . . . *nice*. Not at all like someone who would post a cruel picture online. Harlow had a hard time understanding how Erin could be so nice to "Jean" but so nasty to Harlow. It was like Erin was the one wearing a mask. Except Harlow couldn't figure out which was the real Erin and which one was a disguise.

Now Harlow felt she'd missed her chance to confront them. And . . . was it so wrong to try to forget about the picture, just for a while? Why couldn't she enjoy being Jean for a little longer? Maybe she'd never take her mask off. Maybe after the carnival she'd just disappear, like a ghost.

"Hey," Lulu said suddenly. "Is that Audrey up there? She's been gone a long time—I thought she went to get food or something?"

Up in the middle of the stage two girls were twirling fiery batons. Now that she was paying attention, Harlow recognized Audrey's curly red hair, which flew in all directions as she spun around in a circle.

"What a show-off," Erin grumbled.

"I can't *believe* she didn't tell me she was going to be part of the show," Julia huffed.

A woman in the row in front of them twisted around and snapped, "Can you girls keep it down?"

"Maybe she wanted to surprise us?" Lulu said, ignoring the woman, but she was quickly silenced by a withering glare from Julia. "I mean," she added quickly, "we all know how much Audrey likes to be the center of attention."

We do? Harlow thought. *How do we know that?* But then Harlow had a delicious thought: Jean *wouldn't* know that. Jean wouldn't know anything at all about Audrey, Julia, or the circle of friends who'd deserted Harlow last year. She could ask whatever she wanted.

"Aren't you and Audrey best friends?" Harlow whispered to Julia, and then winced, thinking maybe that was too direct of a question. Right then she was extremely grateful for her costume and the raspiness of her voice.

Julia got really quiet as Erin and Lulu waited for her to answer. Harlow waited too. She was genuinely curious. Once upon a time Harlow, Audrey, and Grace had been inseparable. Then the fire happened. Grace sunk into a melancholy silence and Harlow was ostracized. That left Audrey, who in the sudden absence of her two closest friends spent more and more time with Julia. If you studied the pictures they posted online—which Harlow did multiple times a day—you'd think they were not just best friends, but sisters.

Their group was silent as everyone waited for Julia to answer. Harlow wondered what Erin and Lulu were thinking. She figured either of them would relish the chance to take Audrey's place and become Julia King's new best friend.

"I don't have a best friend," Julia said, beaming around the group. "You're all my best friends."

They turned their attention back to the show, and after a few more minutes, Erin held up her phone and said, "Look."

On the screen was a picture someone had posted of Audrey spinning her fiery baton, sparks shooting off into the darkness. Somewhere out in the crowd their classmates were posting pictures of her online, making Audrey's debut as a circus performer more than real, captured online for everyone to see. Through the whitish glare illuminating Julia's face as she stared at the picture, Harlow could see her lips pursed in a frown. Harlow glanced around at the audience, wondering how many of her classmates had snapped pictures of Audrey, and saw Erin's crush, Lucas Carter, chatting with a couple of his friends.

She nudged Erin. "There's Lucas, over in the middle of the second row."

Erin didn't look at the second row. She turned to stare at Harlow. "How do you know his name?"

"Oh, Lulu mentioned it earlier," Harlow said hastily, trying to keep her voice down so Lulu wouldn't hear. She was vaguely aware that the music had ended and a man in a black top hat and red coattails had appeared on the stage and was speaking.

"Earlier when?" Erin asked. She was looking right at Harlow, but not exactly. Harlow had the uncomfortable feeling Erin was actually staring at her mask. Like maybe she was wondering who was underneath it.

"Ladies and gentlemen, can I get a volunteer?" said the man in the black top hat.

Julia stood up. "Let's go," she told them.

Dutifully, everyone rose from their seats, but Harlow began to panic. What did they want the volunteers to do onstage? What if it involved taking off her mask? And besides that, Erin was now casting suspicious glances her way.

While everyone else filed quietly up the aisle behind Julia, Harlow turned and fled the other way toward the exit.

"*I'm sorry, girls,*" said the man in the black top hat. "*But we only need one volunteer. Who will it be?*"

Just before Harlow slipped outside the tent, she heard Julia answer in a clear, loud voice, "Me. Definitely me."

▸ 24 ◂

Audrey

WHILE AUDREY SPUN AND TWIRLED, FLAMES sparking on either end of her baton, the worries that had been pressing on her all night vanished, like they had never been there at all.

On the carousel she had wished something amazing would happen. And here she was, spinning like a professional circus performer! So many times she worried about saying the right thing at school. Wearing the right clothes. Doing all the right things at home—making sure that everything was running smoothly until her mother could come back and take over again. And for just a few moments, it felt good to stop caring about any of it. To do something different and wild and adventurous and fun. To not worry if she was doing the same routine as Lynn—to move and spin and twirl at her own pace.

The music ended and a voice over the loudspeakers called, "*Ladies and gentlemen, can I get a round of applause for our fire twirlers?*" A man holding a microphone stepped onto the stage. He was dressed in a black top hat and red coattails and grinned at the crowd. "*I'm your host tonight, Mr. Electrico. And now, ladies and gentlemen, can I get a volunteer?*"

Lynn began heading backstage. When Audrey went to follow her, Lynn said, "I have to get changed for my next act. Twyla usually performs the Bouquet. Can you cover for her still?"

"Definitely," Audrey said. She was having the time of her life! Plus, she loved flowers. Her mother always used to gather bouquets of wildflowers in the summer.

While Mr. Electrico was choosing a volunteer from the audience, Audrey followed Lynn over to the side of the stage. Lynn grabbed a rack of knives that had been stashed under a blanket and plunked them into Audrey's hands.

"What's this?" Audrey whispered.

"The Bouquet. You can't have a knife throwing contest without knives."

"Knives? But I figured—never mind." Audrey thought for a second. "What am I throwing them at?" She had terrible aim.

Lynn seemed to think she had a wonderful sense of humor, though, because she threw back her head and laughed. "Have fun out there," she called as she slipped backstage.

"And now—will someone bring me the Bouquet?"

Audrey stepped forward and held up the rack of knives. The audience cheered and she smiled widely. For a brief instant she wondered again if her mother was in the crowd, watching her.

She walked the knives over to Mr. Electrico, passing the volunteer from the audience—who turned out to be Julia! Audrey waved, receiving a thin smile from Julia in return, but inside she was disappointed. She thought she'd get to throw the knives, not just carry them out onstage so Julia could throw them.

"Here you go," she said to Mr. Electrico. She turned to head offstage when he stopped her.

"Pssst. Where do you think *you're* going?"

Audrey stopped. "What?"

He pointed to the opposite wall where the outline of a person was drawn in thick white chalk against a black background. "Take your place."

"My place?" Audrey repeated, alarm sounding in her voice. "You mean, you'll be throwing the knives at *me*?"

"*I* won't." He pointed to Julia. "*She* will. She needs a target. . . . Don't look so spooked, Red. It's all fake. She can't hurt you."

Audrey glimpsed the determined look on Julia's face; she wasn't so sure about that. Audrey stepped in front of the chalk outline and spread her arms, hoping she wasn't making the biggest—and possibly the last—mistake of her life.

"Ladies and gentlemen, don't try this at home!"

Mr. Electrico said, and the audience roared with laughter.

Audrey wasn't in a laughing mood. From across the stage she could see Julia, armed with knives, and she didn't look good-natured at all. She looked downright dangerous, and Audrey couldn't help wondering again if Julia was mad at her. She'd been keeping a mental catalog of every single thing she'd done in the last few weeks, and now, as Julia took aim, Audrey mentally flipped through it.

"Ready . . . Aim . . . Fire!"

Julia hurled the knife. It spun end over end, straight toward Audrey . . . until it pulled to the side, landing just outside her elbow. That's when she understood: magnets. Somehow, the knives weren't actually real, but magnets. Mr. Electrico was right; they couldn't hurt her.

After Julia had thrown the last knife, she was dismissed back to the crowd and Audrey bowed to the audience.

Tricia was waiting for her backstage, and she didn't

look happy. "What on earth did you think you were *doing*?" she snapped. "Do you honestly think we let kids join the show?"

"No," Audrey said. "I just, I don't know . . . I just wanted . . ."

"What?" Tricia said. "You just wanted *what*?"

"I just wanted people to see me," Audrey blurted out.

Tricia sighed. "Most people do."

Audrey turned to leave and Tricia called, "Hey, did you find your mother?"

"Not yet," Audrey called back. *Not yet.*

▶ 25 ◀

Grace

GRACE WAS VAGUELY AWARE SHE AND DIEGO were holding hands as they raced through the carnival, but she was too scared to care. She had never disobeyed her mother so blatantly before; she was going to be in so much trouble.

"Where are we going?" Diego yelled.

"I don't know," Grace yelled back.

Grace herself might not have known where they were going, but her feet knew exactly what they were doing. They carried her—still pulling Diego along—

outside the iron gates and the brightly lit grounds of the carnival. Moonlight frosted the wheat fields beyond, turning everything an eerie silver color. The sudden silence and absence of color made it feel like they'd traded one reality for another.

Traveling to an alternate reality was the best explanation for where she found herself now, holding Diego's hand as they slowed down to a walk. A thrill passed through her, and Grace could feel her cheeks beginning to burn. They glanced at each other at the same time and pulled their hands away.

"Do you believe me now?" Diego said quietly as they continued to walk.

"I believe you," Grace said. "How long have they been dating?"

"Not long, I think. They got to talking because they both missed your—" Diego stopped suddenly. "Anyway, they've been going out every Friday night."

"That can't be right." Grace shook her head. "Friday nights my mom goes to her book club."

"Are you sure about that?" Diego asked quietly.

Now that she thought about it, she *wasn't* sure. When was the last time she'd seen her mother actually read a book?

"Maybe not," Grace said, and Diego nodded.

"I'm pretty sure they drive over to Fairvale most Friday nights," he said. "They didn't want anyone in Clarkville to start gossiping about them."

"Or tell me," Grace said.

"Or tell you," Diego agreed. He stopped walking. "Now what? Should we go back to the carnival?"

Just then Grace's phone began ringing. She didn't have to check the screen; she knew it had to be her mother. Nobody else actually called her; all her friends preferred to text.

"I can't go back, not yet." Grace knew her mother. She'd spend the rest of the evening hunting Grace down. She'd check every ride, break up every clique. She wouldn't rest until Grace was safely back at home, grounded for the rest of her natural-born life.

"So, where to, then?"

"Straight ahead," Grace said, suddenly sure she'd known where they were going the minute she grabbed Diego's hand.

"What's straight—" He stopped and looked at her when he understood. "Are you sure?"

"I'm sure," Grace said.

The wheat field came to an end and the ground sloped sharply upward. On the other side of the hill, like it had been waiting for them all night, were the remains of the Carlson Factory. She began striding down the hill, Diego following behind her.

She hadn't been here since before the night of the fire. There wasn't much left now. Just charred wood and blackened steel and thick marks scarring the ground. In Grace's mind it all ignited with a loud *pop*, orange embers shooting into the night, and for a brief moment she wondered what the fire *really* looked like last year.

Because of course she hadn't been there. She's been asleep in her own bed, unaware her life was going to change forever.

"I heard Mr. Carlson has people in town tonight," Diego said as they both stared at the wreckage. "That he might be getting closer to getting it rebuilt."

Grace wanted to say she didn't care if it ever reopened. The factory was the reason why she'd lost her father, and as far as she was concerned the ground they were standing on could remain a pile of ash and busted steel forever.

But the world kept turning—even when you didn't want it to—and Grace knew a lot of families in Clarkville were hurting.

Broken glass littered the grounds, glistening in the moonlight, and they picked their way through it carefully until they came upon an old padlocked steel trunk. It was charred now, but still intact.

"Wow," Diego said, crouching level with the trunk. "What do you think is inside?"

Grace lowered herself beside him. "I know what's inside."

Unfortunately, neither of them had experience with picking locks; instead, Grace picked up a big rock and raised it over her head. "Here goes nothing," she said.

Three strikes later and the lock was out. Grace lifted up the top of the trunk and removed a bat, a mitt, and a baseball.

"Whoa," Diego said. "What's all this?"

"Mr. McKinley's old sports equipment," Grace said. "He kept it in his office for Audrey, me, and Harlow to play with." And play with it they had, until Audrey and Harlow lost interest. Back before Harlow became popular. Before boys became, well, *boys*, and everyone got a cell phone and everything began to change. Back when both Mr. McKinley and Mr. Carlson seemed like second and third fathers to her and their families spent tons of time together.

"Want to play?" Grace asked.

"What—you mean right *now*?" Diego asked.

"Yeah—just for a few minutes. You pitch and I'll bat!"

"Well . . ." Diego looked back at the carnival.

"Please?" Grace said quickly. "I promise we won't be that long."

With one more glance over his shoulder, Diego said, "Okay, sure."

They walked out onto the factory's parking lot—a couple weeds were sprouting from cracks in the pavement—and Grace handed Diego the ball and the baseball glove. "Let's see what you've got!" she said.

Turned out he didn't have much. Like his father, Diego was a lousy pitcher. Each time he threw the ball, Grace cracked it over his head and he'd have to go chasing after it. Grace ran too, imagining herself flying past first base, then second, then third. As she ran, something caught her eye where the parking lot met the edge of the factory grounds. Among the silvery shards of broken glass Grace saw something winking gold. She stopped and crouched down to get a better look, and a thrill passed through her when she realized what it was—a Clarkville state championship baseball ring. It was sitting in a pile of ashes, as shiny as ever, like it had never been touched by the fire. Grace held it up to the moonlight and squinted. There it was—an inscription on the inside. *HC* for Henry Chang. It was her dad's ring, missing for nearly a year.

Grace slid it onto her finger. It was far too big, and the metal felt cool on her skin. She remembered the pride on her dad's face when he talked about the state championship game, and how it meant even more to him because he got to share it with his two best friends: Russ Carlson and Jimmy McKinley.

"What's that?" Diego said, coming up behind her.

"Something my dad left behind," Grace murmured. And something Grace would have had to leave behind—a piece of her dad's story—if she hadn't found it. But here it was now in her trembling hands, like the carousel had decided to grant her wish.

If the carousel could grant one of her wishes, could it grant a second?

"Let's go back," Grace said.

"Okay." Diego nodded.

"I need to figure out a way to avoid my mother," Grace said as they turned around and began walking back.

"Why?" Diego asked.

"Because I'm grounded—I wasn't supposed to go to the carnival."

Diego pursed his lips and thought for a second. "I could text all my friends and tell them to keep an eye out for our parents—kind of like our own reverse spy service. If we know where they are, then we know where *not* to go."

"I like it," Grace said, as they began climbing the hill again. "I need to stay at least until midnight."

"Why midnight?" Diego asked.

Grace almost told him about the pumpkin gram right then, but she didn't. She wanted to hold onto the fantasy for a little bit longer in her imagination—that when she showed up to the Ferris wheel at midnight Diego would be standing there waiting for her and tell her he had sent it. But she knew he hadn't.

Still, Grace figured it never hurt to dream a little.

Harlow

2 HOURS TO MIDNIGHT

AFTER LEAVING THE SHOW, HARLOW DECIDED to take a few more photos of the carnival. She captured a couple great moments: A cute couple licking the sides of a dripping ice-cream cone; a puppeteer making his marionette dance while a bunch of children looked on.

Just as she finished snapping a photo of a mime talking on his cell phone, a couple of Harlow's class-mates walked by. The also had their phones out. "I'll bet Harlow Carlson picks her nose all the time," one of them said, and the rest laughed. Harlow, forgetting for a second that she was wearing her mask, instinctively turned away so they wouldn't see her.

She dreaded showing up to school on Monday morning. Maybe she'd ask her mother if she could stay home sick. Or maybe she'd show up to school in her mask and never take it off ever again. If everyone thought her real face was so ugly, maybe she'd just wear a fake one for the rest of her life.

"Step right up," a carnie standing in front of a board of inflated balloons said after she snapped a picture of him. "Five bucks gets you seven darts. Pop seven balloons and you'll win a prize."

"Dare you to pop all seven," said a voice in her ear. Ethan.

"Hi!" Harlow said as she paid for the darts. "Are you puke-free now? Or should I keep my distance?"

"That's funny," Ethan said. "Real hilarious."

Harlow shrugged. "It's not my fault you ate all those chili fries."

"It is, actually. You dared me to do it."

"And you just automatically say yes to every dare?"

Harlow said, although she already knew that was mostly true. That's partly why Ethan got in trouble so much. She threw three darts in quick succession. *Pop, pop, pop!* "What if someone dared you to jump off a bridge?" she asked.

He grinned. "Depends on how tall the bridge was."

"Real smart, Ethan," she said, throwing another three darts. "That's a stellar intellect you've got there." She threw her last dart, popping another balloon. "Yes! That's number seven!" She turned to him, her arms raised triumphantly, but he was staring back at her, a suspicious look in his eyes.

"How did you know that?" he asked.

"How did I know what?"

"My name. How did you know my name?"

"What? Oh . . ." Harlow thought fast. "You told me before we rode the Clown Faces."

He shook his head. "I'm pretty sure I didn't. I know I didn't."

"Oh, um . . . I think I asked one of the girls your name."

"Oh yeah?" His eyes brightened with interest. "You asked about me?" Was Ethan trying to flirt with her? Because if he was . . . well, to be honest, it felt nice and she didn't want it to stop. Harlow had missed him this past year, almost as much as she had missed Audrey and Grace.

"I only asked about you," Harlow said, "because I've never seen someone puke so much before."

He grinned. "What can I say? I'm gifted."

The carnie manning the game booth—who looked like he'd been waiting for Harlow and Ethan to stop talking—held out a box. "Pick your prize," he told Harlow.

She selected a tiny stuffed panda bear, then they both turned away and began walking, falling into step with each other. It was like they'd suddenly decided to spend some time hanging out together.

"Where are your friends?" Harlow asked.

Ethan shrugged. "Who knows? We split up earlier, and I haven't seen them since."

As they walked, they passed by the Ferris wheel. Harlow had just enough time to wonder about the pumpkin gram she'd received before she heard Mr. McKinley's voice call, "Ethan! Ethan, over here! I need to talk to you!"

The change that came over Ethan was immediate. His grin vanished. His jaw tightened. And his shoulders tensed.

"What's wrong?" Harlow asked.

"That's my dad," Ethan said as they both turned and walked toward the Ferris wheel. "What?" he said shortly when they reached Mr. McKinley, who was manning the control box.

"Have you seen Grace or her mother tonight?" he asked.

"Not since earlier," Ethan answered. "Why?"

Harlow hadn't seen Mr. McKinley up close since she visited him in the hospital the day after the fire. He looked so much older now. He'd lost a lot of weight. His hair had turned gray, and his green eyes weren't as bright as Harlow remembered, but dimmer. He looked like a ghost of his former self.

"I heard they're moving. If you see them, I want you to offer our help."

"Dad—the *last* person they'd accept help from is you."

Mr. McKinley's face seemed to collapse in on itself, and he went back to the ride controls. "I just wanted to help," he said, so softly Harlow wasn't sure she heard right.

Ethan whipped around and stomped off. Harlow jogged until she caught up with him.

"That was mean," she said.

"How would you know?" he said, taking long strides. "You're not from around here. You wouldn't understand."

But Harlow thought she *did* understand. She'd heard the rumors about Mr. McKinley. How he couldn't be counted on to take care of his kids now that Audrey's mom had left. How his Chevy rolled into their driveway at the crack of dawn because he'd been out all night. How a few people had seen Audrey shopping for groceries at the general store, scratching her head as she read the directions off a box of mashed potatoes.

Harlow was tempted to take her mask off and tell Ethan what her own father used to say about Mr.

McKinley, before the fire tore their friendship apart: that Jimmy McKinley was not only one of his best friends in the world, but one of the hardest workers he'd ever met, too.

Almost as if he could read her thoughts, Ethan said, "He's changed a lot this year, is all."

Yeah, Harlow thought as they continued walking, *I guess we've all changed.*

Grace

THE CARNIE STANDING IN FRONT OF THE iron gates wouldn't let them back inside the carnival.

"Where are your tickets?" he asked.

"We already handed them over," Grace said. "We've been here for hours; we just left for a little while."

"Did you get your hand stamped when you left?"

"No—we were in a hurry." Grace's phone rang again, and she finally just shut it off. Her mother kept calling her, but Grace was determined to avoid speaking to her until after midnight.

"Without a stamp there's nothing I can do. Not unless you want to buy another ticket."

"Come on," Diego said. "Can't you just let us back in? It's late—people are starting to leave."

Diego was right; families laden with carnival prizes were streaming out the gates, pulling bleary-eyed children along in their wake.

Grace turned to Diego. "Do you have any money?"

"Some, but not enough for another ticket."

"Same here." Grace kicked the ground in frustration; she couldn't help but think she was running out of time. How this was her last night in town and the clock was ticking down, first to midnight and to whatever she'd find at the Ferris wheel; but also to tomorrow morning, when her current life, the only life she'd ever known in Clarkville, was ending.

She *had* to get back inside the carnival. There was no way she was missing out. She was going to be at the Ferris wheel at midnight, even if that meant sneaking back into the carnival. Maybe they could make a break for it and just run back inside? She stared at the carnie and wondered if she and Diego could outrun him. This late in the night, how long would he spend trying to find two kids?

A small boy who'd been exiting the carnival with his family lost his grip on a large bag of water he'd been carrying. It plopped to the ground and opened, water splashing everywhere. "My prize goldfish!" he cried.

Both his parents lunged to the ground to retrieve the beached goldfish and his father cried, "Does anyone have any water?"

The carnie who'd been guarding the gates had a half-empty water bottle in his hands, and he rushed over to help them.

"Let's go!" Grace said, and they sprinted past the gates and into the carnival. They wove their way through the crowd, Diego holding his phone out in front of them like a tracking device. Diego's friends had taken his request to heart, and they were gleefully texting him the location of their parents as they hunted for Grace and Diego:

they're by the Zipper

Go Diego! Go Grace!

by the carousel

they look SO mad

you guys are dead

Now they're checking the snack emporium

they just walked through the iron gates to check the parking lot

"I think we've got a little time," Diego said after he'd read the last text aloud, and Grace agreed. The parking lot was a good walk from the iron gates past a windswept field to a large plot of packed dirt.

"Want to go on a ride?" Diego said. They were passing the Fun Slide; striped in bright shades of primary colors, it looked like a gigantic stick of gum reaching out to grab them. Before Grace could respond, her stomach made another loud, embarrassing gurgle.

"Still hungry?" he said.

"Yeah. Starving, actually." They'd left their bag of popcorn, mostly uneaten, back inside the velvet tent when they'd first run away from their parents.

"I think we've got enough money to split a snack," Diego said.

They made their way to the Snack Emporium, where Grace finally tried to buy the funnel cake she'd been hoping for all night.

But unfortunately, some things just weren't meant to be.

"We're out," said the carnie manning the stand.

"Out? How can you be out of funnel cakes?" Grace said.

He shrugged. "They're really popular. You should have bought one earlier."

They bought a plate of onion rings instead, which Diego carried to a wooden bench near the back of the Snack Emporium. "Dig in," he said. Grace stared at him while he squirted an enormous amount of ketchup and mustard on their plate and began to eat.

Grace hated ketchup. And mustard. But tonight, she didn't care. Sitting across from Diego, sharing a plate of onion rings—it was almost like a date!

But on a date you were supposed to talk to the other person. She wracked her brain, trying to think of something to say. "Did you catch the Cubs game on

Wednesday?" she asked. It had been a spectacular game; they'd been down one run and then tied it up at the bottom of the ninth, then won in overtime. Grace was dying to talk about it with someone—Julia and Erin and Lulu couldn't care less—and she hoped Diego would be that someone.

Except he was shaking his head. "I'm not really into baseball," he said.

Not "into" baseball? This was extremely disappointing news. And confusing too. Who didn't like baseball?

Still, Grace figured no one—not even Diego Martinez— was perfect, so she decided to push on. "Have you been having a good time tonight?" she asked.

"The best!" he answered, and Grace jerked back slightly. His breath was really oniony.

"What have you liked so far about it?" Grace winced. Was that a stupid question? Making conversation with the boy you liked was turning out to be *hard*.

"The best part is right now," Diego answered, and Grace's heart began to pound.

"It is?" she said.

"Yeah. It's like we're fugitives on the run and—" He broke off and his eyes widened. "Don't turn around," he said. "Our parents just walked into the Snack Emporium—*I said don't turn around!*"

"Sorry." Grace had only briefly glanced over her shoulder, but it was enough to catch a glimpse of her mother's multicolored hair.

"Wow," Diego said. "Your mom looks *really* mad."

"Mad or sad?" Grace asked. Mad, she could handle. But she would feel awful if she'd made her mom sad tonight.

"Mad." Diego nodded. "Oh, yeah. *Definitely* mad."

"What should we do?" Grace asked.

"She's looking right this way," Diego said, dropping his gaze quickly.

Grace tensed. "Do you think she's seen us?"

"No—a couple mimes just moved behind you. They're acting sort of like a shield."

Grace was fighting the urge to turn around and look. She knew if she did, her mother would catch sight of her like a tractor beam. Then the night would be over.

"Okay, here's what we're going to do," Diego said. "When I say 'now,' we're going to get up and quickly walk the other way."

While he continued to watch their parents, Grace slowly swung her legs free of the wooden bench and perched on the edge, waiting.

"Not yet . . . Not yet . . . Okay, they're starting to turn away. They're turning—Now!"

And they were off, sprinting from the Snack Emporium and deeper into the carnival. Their parents must have seen them, though, because Grace heard pounding footsteps behind her, followed by her mother's voice yelling, "Grace! Get back here!"

▶ 28 ◀

Harlow

HERE'S SOMETHING NOBODY KNOWS: LAST
October, one day before Halloween and one week
before the fire, Ethan asked Harlow to go out with him.
She'd been over at the McKinleys' house—their old
one on Hudson Road—and she and Ethan had gotten
into a daring match while Audrey and Grace watched
a movie with Maddie and Mason. Harlow dared Ethan
to sneak into the garage where Mrs. McKinley kept the
Halloween candy and steal them some. They ate their
share of Snickers bars, and then Ethan dared Harlow to

kiss his pet frog, Rodney. After all that chocolate and sugar, the top of Rodney's head tasted salty.

After that, they got bored and decided to think up a better dare. Harlow pointed to the huge sycamore tree in the backyard, the one that seemed to stretch all the way up to the clouds, and said, "Dare you to climb all the way to the top."

"I dare *you*," Ethan had answered. "Last one to the top is a rotten egg!"

Harlow wasn't worried; she climbed like a spider monkey, there was no way she'd be the rotten egg.

As it turned out, no one was a rotten egg. They reached the highest branch at the same time. Standing there, clinging to the top of the tree trunk, the leaves of the sycamore whispering all around them, Ethan said, "Will you go out with me?"

While Harlow was considering her answer, the back door banged open and Audrey's voice floated up to them, *"Ethan? Harlow? Are you guys out here?"*

Harlow wondered how Audrey would feel if she started going out with her twin brother.

"Ethan? Harlow?"

"I'll think about it," Harlow had whispered to Ethan.

But not too long afterward, their families weren't speaking to each other anymore.

Harlow hadn't forgotten that night almost a year ago at the McKinleys. How it felt when she and Ethan stood at the top of the sycamore tree, seemingly suspended in the sky, staring at each other. Maybe that was why, after walking around the carnival for a while, when they came up to the Mirror Maze she said, "Let's race. First one through the maze wins. Come on, I dare you. I've always been faster than you!"

She was on the tips of her toes, poised and ready to go, but Ethan stood back and stared at her for a long moment. "Always been faster than me?" he repeated. "I've got another dare. I dare you to take your mask off."

"No," Harlow said. "Anything but that."

"Come on. We both know your name isn't Jean," he said. "Is it?"

Something about the way he said it and the way he was looking at her made her whisper, "No. It's not."

He nodded. "I didn't think so. So, who are you?"

Slowly she removed her mask. "Someone you don't like very much."

"I never said I didn't like you, Harlow." Ethan didn't look too surprised to see her.

They stood staring at each other, the lights of the Mirror Maze flashing above them, until Harlow said, "You stopped talking to me."

"No. *You* stopped talking to *me*." Ethan plunged his hands into his pockets. "Nothing's been the same since last year. Everything feels so messed up."

"It does," Harlow agreed softly. "It really does."

At that very moment, out of the corner of her eye, she saw Julia and the other girls—minus Grace and Audrey—approaching. "I can't believe you got to throw *knives* at her!" Erin was saying.

Quickly, Harlow turned away, but it was too late—she'd been spotted.

"Jean!" Erin called. "Do you want to go through the maze with us?"

Harlow had her back to them. She was struggling to

put her mask back on, but it had snagged on her wig. The girls were only a few feet away—any minute now they'd see her face.

"I've got to go!" she whispered to Ethan.

She dashed into the maze. The girls followed after her, laughing, thinking it was a game.

"Jean! We're coming to get you!"

Mirror to mirror she fled, but everywhere she looked it was her face reflected back at her. First there were two Harlows. Then four, now eight. Her reflection kept multiplying until it seemed she was being chased by a whole army of Harlows.

She ran, twisting and turning through the maze as fast as she could, fighting tears. She never should have tried to fool everyone. She saw that now. She'd made a huge mistake. The minute she'd first run into Erin she should have taken off her mask and said, "I'm not from out of town. I'm Harlow." True, Erin would have slithered away like she'd just crossed paths with a black cat and none of this crazy, wondrous night would have happened. But Harlow also wouldn't be fleeing now, like a rat literally stuck in a maze—a mirrored one—hoping to elude her pursuers.

But, she reminded herself, they were just chasing her, thinking it was all in fun. It wasn't like they were armed with torches and pitchforks.

Maybe not, but they *were* armed with their phones, and Harlow didn't relish the idea of more nasty pictures of her going up online.

She rounded a corner—and smacked right into her own reflection. She'd reached a dead end. Before she could turn around, the girls were behind her.

"Hi, Jean . . . ," Erin said, her voice trailing off as she caught sight of Harlow's face in the mirror.

It was like someone flipped a switch. One minute the girls were giddy and smiling. The next they were staring, blank-faced, at Harlow.

"Harlow," Julia said. "All this time—that was *you?*"

Slowly, Harlow turned around. "Yes," she said. "It's me."

"Wait, I don't get it," Lulu said, frowning. "Jean is really Harlow?"

Julia wasn't frowning. She was deathly calm. "You must think we're idiots," she said. "I mean, that *is* why you tried to play such a nasty trick on us, right?"

"No," Harlow said quickly. "I don't think that. And I wasn't playing a trick on you."

"So . . . you *didn't* hang out with us all night, pretending to be someone else?"

"Yes, but it was just a mistake. Erin asked me if I was from out of town—"

"Oh, so now this is *my* fault?" Erin said.

"No! I just thought it might be nice to spend time with you guys."

"Spying on us, you mean?" Erin said. The three of them were coming closer, forming a half circle around Harlow.

"No! I just missed everyone," Harlow said. She backed up a couple steps and felt the mirror press against her back. "I wasn't trying to spy on anyone, I swear." She turned to Julia. "I just wanted to hang out. You have to believe me. I was serious; I really did want to help you do a sleepover since your party was canceled. I just wanted things to be like how they used to—"

"Wait," Lulu interrupted. "Julia—your party is canceled?"

Another switch flipped. Erin and Lulu weren't looking at Harlow anymore. They were staring at Julia . . . and Harlow understood she'd just made a serious mistake. One that was much bigger than dressing up and pretending to be someone else.

Julia looked at Harlow. She no longer looked calm; her eyes were filled with fury. "I need to talk to my friends," she said.

"Julia—I am so sorry. I didn't mean—"

"Harlow," Julia said, enunciating each word carefully. "Go. Away. *Now*."

Harlow did as she was told.

29

Audrey

1 HOUR TO MIDNIGHT

ONCE UPON A TIME A COUPLE YEARS AGO, Audrey, Harlow, and Grace ran away from home.

Well, they weren't *actually* going to run away from home. They were just going to ride the city bus until they crossed the state line. Ethan had dared Harlow to do it earlier that day, and Harlow wanted some company on her newest adventure. They didn't get very far, though. They only made it to Fairvale before they were caught by Henry Chang, who radioed all his friends at the Fairvale fire and police departments. When they'd gotten off the bus, a fire tanker was there, waiting to escort them back home. Audrey, who'd been nervous the whole bus ride, had felt enormously relieved when she'd seen the big red truck.

But now, after walking around trying to find everyone, Audrey definitely didn't feel relieved when she found Julia standing by herself near the Mirror Maze. Audrey couldn't put her finger on it, but something seemed . . . *wrong*, somehow. Julia looked like she was angry about something. An angry Julia King was never a good thing.

"Hi," Audrey said as she approached.

Julia looked over. "Hi," she said.

"Is everything okay?" Audrey asked.

"Tonight has been so dumb," Julia huffed, and something about the way she said it made Audrey go on high alert.

"Where are the others?" she asked. Right then she didn't want to be alone with Julia.

"Lulu's parents just picked her up. Erin wanted to ride the Tilt-A-Whirl again before she had to leave. Grace is off somewhere with Diego Martinez—I don't know where because she's not bothering to answer my texts."

Audrey was tempted to say she knew how annoying that could be—especially since Julia hadn't been answering *her* texts all night, but she held her tongue.

Julia fixed Audrey with an imperious stare. "So, you decided to join the carnival? Well?" she prompted, crossing her arms when Audrey didn't answer right away.

Audrey blew out a breath. So Julia *was* mad. She should have seen that coming. Julia never liked being upstaged, and right now Audrey was occupying everyone's attention. Online, anyway. Right after she'd left the velvet tent, Audrey had checked her phone and found a ton of pictures posted of her twirling her fire baton! She'd gotten five new followers, which meant she'd reached three hundred first. She'd won, which meant Julia had lost.

"I didn't join the carnival," Audrey said.

"Oh really? Looked that way to me."

"I didn't—I was getting Grace's funnel cake, like you *asked* me to, remember? And I just got a little sidetracked."

"A *little*?" Julia repeated. "More like a lot."

Audrey said nothing. When Julia got mad like this, she'd found it was best to be quiet and just wait it out.

"You know you're my best friend, right?" Julia said suddenly.

I don't know, are we? Audrey thought to herself. Before tonight she would have said so. But what is a best friend? A *real* best friend? Someone you have to text to receive permission to wear your favorite sweater? Someone you would take a million selfies with, but never in a million years would you tell them how hard life feels sometimes?

"You didn't invite me to your birthday party," Audrey blurted.

Julia frowned. "What?"

"Your birthday party—you've been talking about it all day, and you said you could only bring two people. But you never actually said I was invited."

Julia stared at her for a long time, seemingly thinking very hard. Was it that difficult for her to decide whether or not to take her *best friend* to her own birthday party?

Finally, Julia seemed to come to a decision. "You're invited," she said. "We're best friends, and you're invited. Okay?"

"Sure," Audrey said. But she wasn't feeling sure about anything right now. "We're best friends."

"Right," Julia said. "And best friends do favors for each other, don't they?"

"Definitely," Audrey said. "I have a huge list of favors you could do for me." She was trying to be funny, but Julia didn't seem to get the joke. Instead she gave Audrey a dirty look. Audrey figured she'd better get right down to it: "What do you want me to do?"

Julia didn't miss a beat. "I want you to send a text to Harlow," she said.

"What?" Audrey said, surprised. "Why can't *you* text her?"

"Because," Julia answered.

"Because why?" Audrey pressed, and Julia stuck her hands on her hips.

"Look—do you want to help me out or not?" she said.

Behind Julia, a puppeteer was making his marionette dance while a crowd looked on. Audrey watched him, her stomach churning. Something didn't seem right about all this. Julia wasn't speaking to Harlow—so now, all of a sudden, why did she want Audrey to text her?

"What do you want me to say?" Audrey asked finally.

Julia grinned. "Tell her you want her to take a ride on the Ferris wheel."

"The Ferris wheel?" Audrey felt her heart begin to pound. Above them the lights from the Mirror Maze had begun blinking, casting shadows on Julia's face, and Audrey couldn't help thinking: *What if?* But then she had another thought: "Harlow isn't even here tonight."

"Oh, trust me," Julia said, a fire in her eyes. "She's here—and I want her to ride the Ferris wheel."

"What time should I tell her to ride it?" But even as she asked, Audrey felt sure she already knew the answer.

"Midnight," Julia said.

"Um . . ." Audrey stalled, trying to figure it out. Julia wanted her to send a text to Harlow to ride the Ferris wheel. At midnight. Was it possible that *Julia* had sent the mysterious pumpkin gram? But if so, why hadn't she ever said anything to Audrey? And what did any of it have to do with Harlow?

And why did *she* have to be the one to send the text? If Julia wanted Harlow to ride the Ferris wheel at midnight, why couldn't she text Harlow herself?

Actually, Audrey was pretty sure she knew the answer to that one.

Every time Grandma McKinley got mad and said a bunch of bad words (which was quite frequently, especially during baseball season) she said a Hail Mary. As far as Audrey could tell, saying a Hail Mary meant you said a bunch of good words and then you'd be forgiven for whatever bad things you'd done.

Audrey figured texting Harlow for Julia was sort of the same thing. Audrey had done a bad thing. She'd allowed great pictures of herself to be posted online and she'd reached three hundred followers before Julia, meaning Julia had come in second.

Julia did not like coming in second.

So now Audrey would have to do this one small favor

for Julia. Then afterward everything would be okay again and things could go back to normal.

The question was, did she *want* things to go back to normal? What was normal anyway? Nothing had seemed normal in the last year. And nothing would ever be normal, not ever again. Grace was moving tomorrow, and Audrey hadn't even said goodbye. She'd planned to tonight, even though she'd known it would be awkward. But instead she'd spent most of the night chasing a stranger in a pirate costume or standing in line for a stupid funnel cake.

Audrey was having a hard time remembering why everyone stopped talking to Harlow last year. But she missed Harlow—and Grace. She missed watching Cubs games at the Carlsons house or doing her homework with Grace and Harlow on the floor of her father's office at the Carlson Factory.

Julia, who seemed to have had enough of Audrey's stalling, turned away. "Text me after it's done," she said as she headed in the direction of the Tilt-A-Whirl. Audrey understood she wasn't to follow. Not until she obeyed.

The puppeteer was still putting on a show. The marionettes were still dancing on their strings. And something that was foggy and filmy finally solidified in Audrey's mind: She was sick of doing favors for Julia. Plus, she didn't trust her, and hadn't for some time. Audrey had no idea why Julia wanted Harlow at the Ferris wheel at midnight, or if it had anything to do with the pumpkin gram, but she wanted no part of it.

"No!" Audrey called to Julia's retreating figure.

Julia turned around. "What did you say?"

"I said no. I'm not doing it."

Audrey turned away and started walking. Somewhere at the carnival was a woman in a pirate costume who looked a lot like her mother. She was going to find her.

30

Grace

THEY RAN—THIS TIME NOT HOLDING HANDS—twisting this way and that through the crowd until the sound of their parents calling their names died away. Diego led them to the farthest edges of the carnival, beyond the carousel, to a darkened tent with a sign on it that read **OUT OF ORDER**.

"In here," Diego said. "Quick, before they see us again."

They ducked inside, and Grace said, "Where are we?"

Beyond the tent flaps was a dirt walkway and a small pond. Colorful lanterns crisscrossed above. Piles of wooden boats and fishing rods were stacked near the tent wall.

"It's a ride," Diego answered. "Fishing for Fortune."

"Fortune?" Grace said. "You mean like a fortune cookie?"

"Sort of. I heard a few people talking about it—a bunch of the boats broke earlier so they had to shut the whole thing down. You row a boat into the middle of the water and hook a fortune with the fishing pole."

Grace stared at the pond. The water seemed lit with a warm, golden glow. "You mean there are a ton of fortunes down there, just waiting to be found?" Her gaze strayed to a solitary wooden boat sitting near the edge of the water.

Diego grinned. "Just waiting to be found," he repeated.

While Diego dragged the wooden boat into the water, Grace grabbed a couple fishing rods. They clambered into the boat and rowed to the middle of the pond. Grace cast her line and waited. How would she know when she'd caught her fortune?

A few seconds later her pole jerked slightly. "I've got something!" She reeled the line in. Attached to the hook was a glittery golden egg—sort of like a plastic Easter egg with a loop on top. She cracked it open; inside was a tiny scroll, which she quickly unrolled and read:

You have something in your teeth.

Diego burst out laughing, and at first Grace thought maybe he'd read her fortune. But when she looked she saw he had an egg and a scroll of his own, which he showed to Grace.

Never eat beans before you go on a date.

"Someone's got a sense of humor," he said. "Good thing I didn't eat any beans!" he added.

Grace laughed, then wondered: Did that mean he considered *this* a date?

She cast her line again, and this time, the fortune she received was more serious:

It's up to you to create the moment you want.

Grace knew what she wanted. She wanted her magical carnival story. She wanted to kiss Diego on her last night in Clarkville. For the first time, she thought maybe that wasn't something she simply *hoped* could happen; maybe it was something she could *make* happen.

Her phone pinged with a text. It was yet another one from Julia, who kept texting her:

Are you still with Diego?

Grace ignored it and tried to think of something to say to Diego. Why couldn't talking to boys be easier?

"Did you ride the carousel tonight?" she blurted suddenly.

"No," Diego said. "I don't like carousels."

"Oh," Grace said, trying not to show her disappointment. She'd hoped they could share each other's wishes.

"You know what ride I really like?" Diego said. "The Ferris wheel."

"Yeah, I like it too," Grace said quickly, deciding to press on. "I also really like the carousel. I rode it and made a special wish. It's stupid, but . . . I wished that—"

She was interrupted by a string of texts exploding from her phone. All of them from Julia.

Where are you?

Your mother is looking for you!

What is going on?

What's Diego saying about me?

WHY WON'T YOU ANSWER MY TEXTS?

"Who keeps texting you?" Diego asked.

"Julia," Grace said absently. "She's been wanting to hang out with you—"

"I know."

"You do?" Grace glanced over at Diego, and saw he was grinning.

And then a truly awful, horrible thought dawned on her. "Do you *like* Julia?" she asked.

31

Harlow

HARLOW HAD LET HERSELF GET DISTRACTED, no doubt about it. Between the thrill of hanging out with her old friends, flirting with Ethan, and the magic of the carnival, she'd spent far too much time pretending to be someone else and not nearly enough time on her project.

But no more. She'd spent the better part of the last hour hiding out in the city council tent and working on her presentation. She'd interviewed several more people who'd stopped by the tent, including Mr. Bradley, who ran the post office; Mr. King, Julia's father; and Mr. Carter (Lucas's dad), who was just finishing up.

"Do you have anything else to add?" Harlow asked, holding up her phone and centering him in the frame.

Mr. Carter nodded. "I'd like to add that Clarkville is a place that takes care of people." He stared directly at the camera. "Invest in us, and we'll invest in you."

Perfect, Harlow thought as she tapped the phone to stop recording. She was definitely using that.

After he left, she got busy arranging and rearranging the photos and videos, trying to put them in an order that would best show those investors how wonderful Clarkville was. She was interrupted by the sound of footsteps and stifled laughter just outside the tent.

"If someone posted a picture like that of me, I would move to another state," said a voice, one that Harlow vaguely recognized.

"Who are you talking about?" said a second voice.

"Harlow Carlson," said the first. "Have you seen the picture of her?"

There was hushed giggling followed by quiet shuffling.

A group of people—three of them, it looked like—had stopped right on the other side of the tent. Harlow could see their shadows, nearly twelve-feet tall, stretching up the tent wall.

"Look!" said the first voice. Harlow couldn't be completely sure, but she thought it belonged to a girl in her history class. Someone who had never spoken to her before.

Great. Now people she didn't even know were talking about her like they knew her. Like both she and that awful picture were just another part of their Friday-night entertainment.

"What did you just do?" said a third voice.

"I posted a comment. See?"

A pause, and then giddy squealing. "That's hysterical! And true, too."

More laughing. On the other side of the tent Harlow closed her eyes and told herself not to check her phone and start reading the comments. Told herself just to stay here for the rest of the night. To keep working on the presentation. To keep hiding.

Then she thought back to the monster in her closet, the one she was so scared of when she was younger. The one that, once she worked up the courage to open the door, turned out not to be real.

Maybe some monsters are only real if you *let* them be real.

Quickly, before she lost her nerve, Harlow slipped outside. There were three of them, just like she thought. The girl from her history class plus two other girls Harlow didn't recognize at all. Far from the twelve-foot giants their shadows had made them seem, they were each quite a bit shorter than Harlow. In fact, thanks to her newfound height, she towered over them. They were so engrossed in their phones they didn't notice her.

Until one of them looked up, the smile on her face vanishing when she saw Harlow.

"Oh," she said, and elbowed the second girl, who looked up and said, "Oh."

The third girl was still laughing, oblivious. "She looks so hideous—" She broke off abruptly when she also finally looked up.

It was lucky for them Harlow didn't have her phone out, ready to snap a picture and capture the moment. Because all three of them were staring at her stupidly, slack jawed and wide-eyed. Harlow wondered if maybe, just for a little bit, they'd forgotten she was a real person, not just a phantom on the Internet.

"We're so sorry," the first girl said, and the other two nodded vigorously.

"It's okay," Harlow said, even though it wasn't. It wasn't okay, not even a little bit. But Harlow really didn't know what else to say to them. They continued to stare at her, and she added, "There are a lot of other things to do tonight than stare at your phone."

"Right, sure," the first girl said. Then all three of them spun on their heels and ran away, glancing briefly over their shoulders like they all thought Harlow might decide to chase them.

Harlow watched them run, a smile pulling at her lips. It was nice to remember what it felt like to hold her head high.

She was feeling so good she didn't immediately

notice that Julia was standing at the entrance to the tent, twisting her hands together like she was working up the courage to step inside. Julia didn't notice Harlow—Harlow could have just walked away and come back to the tent later, after Julia had gone.

Harlow was no longer the girl who would unthinkingly bring a brand-new phone to school and brag about it when her friends were hurting. But she also didn't want to be the girl who kept hiding from everyone. She'd run away from Julia once tonight; she didn't want to do it again.

She strode up to Julia and tapped her on the shoulder. "Hey," she said.

Julia flinched when she looked over and saw Harlow. "Hey," she answered.

"Where's everyone else?" Harlow asked.

Julia shrugged. "Around. Everyone's kind of doing their own thing now."

They stared awkwardly at each other until Harlow said, "What are you doing here?"

"I ran into my dad," Julia answered. "He said you

were doing a project? To help reopen the factory? I just wanted to see if it was true." She paused. "He sounded really hopeful." She swallowed and looked away quickly. "He hasn't always sounded like that this year."

"It's true," Harlow said. "I don't know if it will make a difference, but it's true."

Julia nodded. "I've been really mad at you for a long time," she said softly. She wouldn't look at Harlow as she spoke; her attention was fixed on the Tilt-A-Whirl as it spun around and around in an endless circle. "I even asked Audrey to—" She stopped. "It's stupid. I guess I'm just mad all the time. At everyone."

Harlow had no idea what she was talking about so she decided to remain silent.

"Anyway," Julia finished, and finally looked at Harlow. "Do you think I could help? With the project?"

Harlow paused. "Sure."

"Do you know what I wished for when we rode the carousel?" Julia said suddenly as they turned and headed back into the tent. "That I lived in a big house like yours."

Harlow, startled, took her time answering. "Well," she said slowly, "it's big, but it can also be lonely."

Julia shrugged. "Small houses can also be lonely," she said, and once again, Harlow felt like she was getting a peek behind the curtain.

▶ 32 ◀

Audrey

MIDNIGHT WAS GROWING CLOSER AND THE night was growing colder. The crowd had thinned and the ride lines were much shorter now. The grass underneath Audrey's feet was trampled and littered with bits of trash and popcorn and peanut shells.

She kicked a stray kernel in frustration. *Nothing* was working out the way it was supposed to tonight. She had looped around the carnival several times, but she hadn't seen the woman in the pirate costume. She *had* seen Grace and Diego running away from Mrs. Chang and Mr. Martinez, a sight that made her laugh out loud. She hoped Grace could work up the courage to finally tell Diego how she felt about him.

Audrey checked the clock on her phone. She had a little bit of time to kill before she had to go to the Ferris wheel, so she decided to work on her audition for *Middle School Daze*—that is, if her phone would actually stop freezing up. She figured she'd start with a selfie, so she made her way over to the carousel and stood in front of it. She waited until the ride was stopped— she didn't want it blurred in the picture—and quickly snapped a photo.

Audrey examined it critically. Her pipe cleaner tiara was crooked; she'd have to fix that. In the background the carousel shone brightly as riders exited. At the edge of the frame something caught her eye. . . .

A text from Julia appeared, covering the screen: Can you do me a favor? If you have any good photos of Clarkville can you—

Irritated, Audrey deleted the text before she finished reading. She was through doing Julia favors tonight.

Audrey went back to the photo and enlarged it. In the background, walking away from the carousel, was the woman in the pirate costume.

▶ 33 ◀

Grace

5 MINUTES TO MIDNIGHT

"DO YOU LIKE JULIA?" GRACE REPEATED.

"No," Diego said.

A large wave of relief crested in Grace's heart. "Oh, okay," she said. "You were smiling so I couldn't tell."

Diego shrugged and cast his fishing line. "I guess it's just nice to know someone likes you, isn't it?"

Diego was staring at the pond, and Grace was staring at Diego. From outside the tent she could hear the sounds of faraway laughter, the carousel music, and water lapping at the edges of the pond. She guessed it *was* nice to know that someone liked you.

If they were brave enough to tell you.

Grace did not consider herself to be brave. She had always been the girl who kept all her thoughts to herself. She secretly hoped when she got to California she'd become a girl who spoke all the words inside her. But what if she became that girl tonight?

What if she became that girl *right now*?

"You know," Grace began, as Diego reeled in another golden egg, "when we were supposed to meet at the Kissing Booth, I was sort of happy because—"

"Hey!" Diego said suddenly. "Look at this!" He showed Grace the fortune he'd just opened:

It's now or never.

Grace swallowed; it really *was* now or never. "I was happy because I like—"

"You know what?" Diego interrupted excitedly. "I just had a great idea! We should go to the Kissing Booth."

Grace sat back, confused. Was this her wish, coming true? She fidgeted with her fishing rod. She wasn't even sure Diego liked her back. But if he was asking to go to the Kissing Booth that had to mean he did, right?

"Sure, let's go," Grace said.

After Diego rowed them back he checked his phone—according to his friends, Grace's mom and his dad were near the Zipper, scanning the crowd. Grace checked her own phone, and her heart plunged. It was almost midnight. She shouldn't be going to the Kissing Booth. She should be heading to the Ferris wheel, and finding out who would be waiting for her. But she had a feeling if she left Diego now, she'd be losing her last chance.

Did she *really* believe anyone would be waiting for her at the Ferris wheel?

"Hey, did you hear about how Harlow Carlson tricked everyone?" Diego said as they left the tent.

A finger of ice traced Grace's spine. "Tricked them how?"

"Erin Donoghue ran into a couple of my friends and they texted me—I guess Harlow dressed up in a costume and pretended to be some girl named Jean."

Jean was actually Harlow?

But Grace didn't have time to wonder about it. She had bigger problems. "So, she's *here*?" Grace said, her voice rising. "Harlow's at the carnival?" An alarm was pounding insistently at her brain: *Alert, alert! Danger, danger!*

"I guess. Anyway, do you think at the Kissing Booth we could—"

Grace barely heard him. She was leaving him behind and sprinting to the Ferris wheel as fast as she could.

Midnight. Harlow Carlson.

Grace had been right all along.

▶ 34 ◀

Audrey

AUDREY WASN'T GOING TO LOSE SIGHT OF her this time.

She followed the woman in the pirate costume through the carnival, vaguely aware that it was just about midnight, and that she should be making her way to the Ferris wheel. But, strange as it seemed, that's exactly where the woman seemed to be heading anyway.

The woman passed the Snack Emporium and the Zipper, and Audrey's heart thundered in her chest. There could be no doubt now—the Ferris wheel was squarely in front of both of them. Rising high into the sky, it looked like a shining wheel of color sparkling against the night.

What if it had been *her mother* who sent the pumpkin gram? What if she had come back and that was her way of saying she was sorry?

Audrey would ride the Ferris wheel a hundred times over, scale any height—no matter how much it terrified her—if it could bring her mother back.

The woman removed her pirate hat as she stepped up to the plank leading to the control box and shook out her long red hair—the exact same shade as Audrey's mother's hair. She walked straight to Audrey's dad and gave him a hug. Audrey hurried closer, feeling like she was going to leap right out of her own skin.

Until the woman turned and Audrey got a good look at her.

The face was exactly right—and at the same time, exactly wrong. With a sinking feeling, Audrey realized she'd made a huge mistake.

The McKinley Family Freak Show, where you can get two for the price of one.

"Aunt Lisa?" Audrey said as she drew near. "I thought you were watching Maddie and Mason tonight?"

"Uncle Dan is with them," Aunt Lisa answered, her cheeks rosy with excitement. "When your dad told me the carnies needed a little extra help this year, I got a job too. It's been so much fun! I've been running errands most of the night—but I just got to ride the carousel. I've been waiting all night to do that!"

Aunt Lisa's green eyes sparkled—the exact same shade of green as Audrey's mother's eyes. They were twins, true, but it was still eerie how much the two of them looked alike. Even her voice sounded like Audrey's mom.

"I wish I'd known." Audrey swallowed. "I saw you two hug just now and I thought . . ."

A flash of understanding passed between Aunt Lisa and her father. "Oh, honey," Aunt Lisa said, reaching out and tucking a strand of red hair behind Audrey's ear. "I miss her too."

"Lisa—could you give Audrey and me a moment alone?" her father said.

"Sure," Aunt Lisa said. "My shift ended anyway. I was just saying goodbye."

After she'd gone, Audrey's father said, "You okay?"

Audrey nodded and swallowed the lump in her throat. "I guess I just thought maybe she'd decided to come home."

"Well, actually . . . she *does* want to come home." Her father turned away and stared straight ahead, watching as a couple of carnies ushered a few boys from her history class into a cart. He punched a button and the cart began rising as another one swept forward.

It took a moment for the meaning of his words to sink in. "How would you know that?" Audrey asked. "Have you talked to her?"

He nodded, still staring straight ahead. "She's called a few times."

Audrey thought back to the odd phone calls he'd received the last couple weeks; it must have been her mother on the other end of the line. "Do you know where she is?" He hesitated, and she said, "You do, don't you?"

"She's been staying with a friend in Fairvale." He punched another button on the control console. "We've been talking and working things out."

"Working things out? What does that mean?"

"We've decided to go see someone—a counselor—together. And your mother agreed that she needs to go back to her doctor and start taking her medication again." He smiled, a real, warm smile, and said, "She's a brave woman, your mother."

Audrey wanted to share in his happiness, but instead a numbness that had nothing to do with the chill in the night began spreading through her. All this time, while she was trying to hold things together—to be a makeshift parent to Maddie and Mason—the real parents were sneaking phone calls to each other like a couple of lovesick teenagers.

Each cart of the Ferris wheel was full now, and her

father punched a button and it began to turn; a colorful moon hanging over the rest of the carnival. Audrey and her father watched it spin in silence.

Once the ride came to an end and the carts were being refilled again, her father said, "We've decided she should come home in a couple weeks."

"Oh, *you've* decided?" Audrey said, the numbness suddenly fading. "Are either of you really capable of making a decision?"

"Watch yourself, Audrey," he said, a warning flashing in his eyes. "I know you've taken on more than your fair share these last couple months, but I am still your father."

"A father who stays out all night with his friends," she retorted.

"Is *that* what you think I've been doing?" he said, sounding genuinely surprised. "I've been *working*, Audrey. I told you that."

"You've been working?" she said skeptically. "That's what you keep saying. *Where* have you been working?"

He glanced at her and sighed. "At the poultry plant

in Fairvale. They were in need of a night janitor and a friend of mine who works there got me the job. I didn't want to tell you and Ethan until I knew for sure it would work out. It's hard work—honest work—and they know I used to run the Carlson Factory. They said if I could hang on until after the holidays a management position would probably open up. They encouraged me to apply for it."

"Well," Audrey said, her voice sounding brittle, "it looks like everything is working out just fine then, isn't it?"

Except it wasn't fine. Nothing seemed fine right then. Her mother may have wanted to come home, but she hadn't bothered to call Audrey and tell her so. Neither of her parents had thought to tell her anything.

"I know this comes as a surprise. This is not how I wanted you to find out. Your mom and I were working on the best way to tell you guys. We had planned—"

"Stop," Audrey said. "I don't want to hear it."

She turned away from him, just as another empty cart was sweeping forward. Without thinking, she stepped inside—cutting in front of a short line of people who had been waiting patiently. But no one seemed to care all that much; it was late, and many of them were blearily rubbing their eyes. Even if they had cared, Audrey was too upset to be polite and wait her turn. It was midnight; the sender had asked her to ride the Ferris wheel at midnight, so that's what she was going to do.

The carnie in charge of filling the ride didn't seem to notice that she'd cut in line; he stared at her steadily for a moment before abruptly leaving. When he returned, he had a brown box, about the size of a shoebox, which he slid into her hands. "Here," he said. "I was told to give it to a girl riding alone at midnight."

Her heart began to hammer as she stared down at the package. Was it from the sender?

Just as he shut the door to the cart, she heard pounding footsteps. The door was flung open and Grace threw herself inside. "Don't open that!" she shouted. Then she blinked and said, "Wait, you're not Harlow."

"No." Audrey said. She might have wondered why

Grace had shoved her way into the cart, or why she expected to find Harlow inside, but her gaze was drawn to the wrinkled pumpkin gram Grace was holding. Audrey recognized the block letters and the message written on it. Her eyes widened.

"I received the exact same message," she said.

"I know," Grace answered.

"*How* do you know?" Audrey asked.

Grace took a deep breath. "Because I'm the one who wrote it."

▶ 35 ◀

Grace

MIDNIGHT

IT WAS TRUE. GRACE HAD SENT ALL THREE pumpkin grams. One to Audrey, one to Harlow, and for good measure, one to herself too.

The idea had come to her shortly after she'd overheard Julia and Erin talking in the library about pranking Harlow at the carnival—possibly at midnight. She'd also thought she'd heard them talking about the Ferris wheel, but she couldn't be sure. She'd wanted to say something to Harlow so badly at school. She'd even stopped once when their paths crossed in the halls, but

Harlow didn't see her. Or if she did see her, she didn't acknowledge her. Harlow didn't acknowledge anyone, really. She pushed forward, hunched underneath the weight of both her backpack and everyone's scorn.

Grace had wondered if that was partly her fault. Had she ever spoken up for Harlow? Had she ever told anyone to stop acting like Harlow had the plague? Had she ever said anything to anyone at all?

She had not. She had stayed in her fog, where it was just so much easier not to speak.

She had been thinking about Harlow—and Audrey—a lot lately. She missed her friends and felt bad for how things had gone after the fire. It felt like time was running out to make things right. In just a couple days she'd be leaving for California, where the sun always shone.

Not only did Grace not want to leave Clarkville, she didn't want to leave without talking to Audrey and Harlow one last time.

But would they want to talk to her? After everything that had happened in the last year, if she texted them and invited them to her house, would they come or would they ignore her?

She also wanted to warn Harlow, and then she'd had a brilliant idea: She could send Harlow and Audrey messages on a pumpkin gram asking them to ride the Ferris wheel at midnight. If Grace had heard wrong, great. Maybe she could end the night, her last in Clarkville, on her favorite ride with her two oldest friends. But, if she was right and Julia *was* planning a nasty prank, Harlow wouldn't have to face it alone. Grace had learned many things from her father, and one important thing he'd taught her—the very last thing—was this: You don't leave your friends behind. Not when they're in danger and it's in your power to help them.

Grace had just signed her name to the pumpkin grams when she wondered: Would Harlow or Audrey even bother to show up if they saw Grace's name at the bottom? Grace wasn't sure, so she ripped them up and purchased new ones. This time she wrote in big block letters and left the "From" section blank.

After she'd finished, she'd thought about how she

wanted a magical carnival story. Then she'd purchased one more pumpkin gram and wrote the same message to herself. She hoped it would be a keepsake, something to remember one of the greatest nights of her life.

"I wrote it," she said again to Audrey, who was staring at her, wide-eyed. "Will you ride with me?"

Audrey

"OKAY," AUDREY SAID, DAZED. "I'LL RIDE with you."

She couldn't believe this. She couldn't believe Grace had sent the pumpkin gram and she couldn't believe she was about to ride the Ferris wheel—even though she was terrified of heights. But the whole night had been so strange and unexpected she figured, *Why not?* She'd twirled fire and had knives thrown at her. The Ferris wheel seemed almost tame by comparison. Maybe it wasn't as scary as she'd remembered.

The cart was circular and roomier on the inside than it looked. A sign near her said **CAREFUL: DOOR CAN OPEN!** She gulped and clutched the shoebox to her chest and told herself everything would be okay.

Back at the control booth, her father punched a button that sent the cart moving up into the night—for about fifteen feet, until the wheel came to a sudden stop and their cart began rocking. Audrey gripped the front of her seat; the ground loomed below, shadow-filled and threatening. Then the cart was moving, up another fifteen feet before stopping again.

"Are you okay?" Grace asked.

"I'm fine," Audrey muttered. "I just," she began, right as Grace gave a startled exclamation, "You're afraid of heights! Oh my gosh, Audrey, I'm so sorry! I forgot!"

"It's okay," Audrey said. With all Grace had been through the last year she wouldn't expect her to remember. After all, Grace hadn't even been with her the last time she'd ridden the Ferris wheel. She'd been with Harlow, who had spent the whole terrifying ride telling her funny stories. It had worked, too, until Audrey made the mistake of looking down. That's when the screaming started.

To distract herself, she looked at the brown shoebox and began to lift the lid.

"Don't open it!" Grace slammed her hand down on the top of the box.

Audrey jerked backward. "Why not?" she asked.

"The box is from Julia and Erin for Harlow. It's some sort of prank."

Audrey stared at the box curiously. "What do you think is inside?"

Grace shook her head. "I just know they were talking about a prank at the Ferris wheel at midnight. That's all I know. Knowing Julia and Erin, it's something nasty, though."

Audrey nodded and slid the box away. "You're right— Julia asked me to send Harlow a text asking her to come here." Her cheeks flushed, and she became flustered. "I didn't do it, though." She looked away from Grace and stared at the inky sky as their cart continued to rise, careful not to look down.

"I sent you the pumpkin gram so we could—I don't know—help her somehow, if she showed up. But there was another reason, too." Grace paused. She sounded formal, like this was a speech she'd been practicing.

"Yeah?" Audrey prompted. She needed something else to think about. The carts were full and the ride was starting up. Her stomach dropped as the wheel began to spin.

"I guess I just wanted to say I was sorry," Grace said.

"Sorry?" Audrey said, startled. "For what?"

Grace couldn't meet her eyes. "For not talking to you. For just . . . not being your friend this year."

"You don't need to apologize," Audrey said quietly. "I might have done the same thing."

A heavy silence filled with all the events of the last year settled between them until Audrey suddenly said, "I think sometimes my dad wishes he was the one who died."

Grace flinched. "That's awful," she said.

"I know," Audrey said quietly. And then, because she thought she might've said too much, she added, "I know you're moving tomorrow. But . . . do you think we could text sometimes? I've missed you."

Grace nodded. "I've missed you too," she said quietly.

It was by far the best part of the night. The only thing that would have made it better was if Harlow was there with them. As their cart continued to spin, Audrey looked at the old water tower standing off in the distance and read the sign:

CLARKVILLE
THE PLACE WHERE THE
PEOPLE YOU LOVE LIVE

Audrey realized the carousel had granted her first wish—her mother was coming home. Maybe not in the way Audrey imagined she would, but still, she was coming back. And Audrey thought maybe instead of riding off into that shiny new life she sometimes dreamed of (or tried to create online) she needed to be right here with Grace in her real, messy, imperfect life; facing her fear as they spun beneath a star-strewn sky. She felt grateful.

But then she made a huge mistake.

She looked down.

► 37 ◄

Harlow

MIDNIGHT HAD COME AND GONE AND Harlow was nowhere near the Ferris wheel. That settled it, once and for all: she wasn't going.

As midnight ticked forward, Harlow had thought about leaving the tent and making her way to the Ferris wheel. But she was truly beginning to doubt anyone would actually be waiting for her. And anyway, she and Julia were making great progress on the presentation. They had enough interviews—courtesy of the people stopping by the city council tent—and nearly enough photos.

"How's it coming over here?" Mrs. Carlson said as she approached the makeshift workspace Harlow and Julia had set up at the back of the tent.

"Good. How did things go with the investors?" Harlow asked, and Mrs. Carlson rubbed her shoulder wearily.

"Good, I think, but it's hard to tell. Your dad took them back to their hotel a while ago. They're meeting at eight sharp tomorrow morning—do you think you guys can have it finished by then?"

Harlow nodded. "I'll be up late tonight, but I can get it done," she said, and Mrs. Carlson smiled.

"That's my girl."

After Mrs. Carlson left, Julia held up her phone and said, "What about this one?" Surprisingly, Julia was turning out to be a great source of good photos. Or maybe not so surprisingly, given how often she posted online.

Harlow glanced away from her mother's laptop and looked over at the picture. It was of a row of Clarkville's fire tankers, every single one of them, lining the street in front of the church the Changs attended.

"I snapped it last year on the way to the funeral," Julia said quietly. "I don't know . . . I guess I just thought it was important."

"It is," Harlow said, swallowing. "It's a good picture. Can you text it to me?"

Just then a gust of wind blew, carrying an ear-splitting scream. Harlow abruptly looked up from Julia's phone. There was something familiar about the sound and Harlow rushed out of the tent, Julia following close behind. They were joined by Mrs. Carlson, who said, "What on earth is that *noise*?"

"It sounds like it's coming from the Ferris wheel," said a woman standing nearby, and all of a sudden Julia was grabbing Harlow's arm.

"I did something really bad," she said.

"What?" Harlow looked over and saw that Julia had gone pale.

"The Ferris wheel. I told Erin to get a box—" she began, but couldn't seem to go on.

"What box? Did you send the pumpkin gram?" Harlow asked, because the pieces were starting to come together.

Except they didn't quite fit. "What are you talking about?" Julia said, blinking. "What pumpkin gram?"

Harlow opened her mouth to explain, just as another scream split the air. There was something familiar about it, a scream she'd heard before.

Last year, on the Ferris wheel.

Harlow took off, running away from the tent. Julia was also running, struggling to catch up to Harlow's long strides. "It was just supposed to be a stupid prank," she called.

Harlow ran faster, practically pushing people out of her way. The Ferris wheel came into view. Someone seated in one of the carts was screaming.

Audrey.

Harlow could make out one cart halfway up the wheel that was tipped at an odd angle. The cart was shaking. It was hard to see so far up, but it looked like Audrey was thrashing about, while whoever was sitting next to her—was that Grace?—was sitting very still.

Everything else at the carnival was coming to a halt. Mr. McKinley was furiously punching buttons at the control box. A crowd of onlookers had formed around the ride. More than a few of them had their phones out and were shooting videos. Harlow heard the sound of a siren in the distance and was glad that at least one of them had the sense to call 911 before they started filming.

She came to a stop next to Ethan, who was staring up at the Ferris wheel. "Is that Audrey up there?" she asked.

"Yeah," he answered shakily. "She's terrified of heights. Last year at the carnival she tried to ride it and—"

"I remember," Harlow said. "I was the one riding with her, remember?"

Ethan glanced over at her. "I remember," he said softly.

"What happened?" Harlow said, turning her attention back to the Ferris wheel. "Why isn't it moving?"

"I don't know," Ethan answered. "I just got here too."

"They tried to stop the ride when the girl started screaming," said a man who'd overheard them. "And then it just sort of . . . *jammed*, and their cart got stuck that way."

"They're *stuck*?" Harlow repeated, and the man nodded.

"Make way!" Two firemen carrying a ladder shoved through the crowd to the front of the Ferris wheel and began setting up the ladder. They were quickly joined by Mr. Martinez, who shook hands with them. Behind him was a white-faced Mrs. Chang. "Please get my daughter down," she said.

"We'll be up there in no time," one of the firemen answered. "And then we'll bring her back down, safe and sound."

"That won't work," Harlow whispered to Ethan and Julia. "Grace will climb down . . . But Audrey will never agree to leave the cart—she's too terrified."

Ethan nodded grimly. "I think you're right."

As they watched, the cart tipped further as Audrey let out another scream and continued thrashing. A gasp went up from the crowd below and Julia said, "Somebody has to try to calm her down."

But the only someone up there was Grace—who was quietly grasping the rail of the cart. Every time Audrey flailed, the cart tipped farther, pushing Grace closer to the door. *Was it locked?* Harlow wondered. What would happen if Grace was pushed flat against it? Would it hold her weight—or would it fly open?

Harlow stared at the ladder. It was almost fully extended now; soon one of the firemen would start climbing.

A plan was forming in her mind. It was slightly dangerous—but after all, this was only a ladder, not a tall tree. And she did climb like a spider monkey, didn't she? She began taking off her boots; she always climbed best in bare feet.

"Harlow, *no*," Ethan said. "It's crazy." But he was peeling off his sweatshirt and rolling up his shirtsleeves. "I'm not letting you go up there without me."

Harlow nodded and said, "We need a distraction."

"*I* can distract everyone," Julia spoke up. She caught Harlow's eye. "I owe you—please?"

Harlow nodded, and Julia said, "On the count of three."

The three of them moved in close to the ladder, mindful of the firemen, who were conferring in hushed tones. While Julia counted off, Ethan turned to Harlow and grinned. "I dare you," he whispered.

"No, *I* dare *you*," she answered.

"*Three*," Julia said.

Harlow and Ethan leaped one after the other onto the ladder and began climbing.

"Hey, you kids!" called one of the firemen. "What do you think you're doing? Get down from there!"

Down below, Harlow heard Julia say, "I don't feel so well." Then there was a sharp gasp, followed by, *"She's fainting!"* and *"Grab her head!"* and *"Everyone stand back and give her air!"*

Harlow smirked and kept climbing; Julia could be an excellent actress when she wanted to be.

"Don't try this at home, kids," Ethan said as they climbed.

"Ethan, Harlow!" came Mrs. Chang's panicked voice. "Come down from there!"

Harlow glanced down. Grace's mother was standing with Diego Martinez's dad, looking like *she* was about to faint. Just underneath Audrey and Grace's cart,

Mr. McKinley was organizing a group of men—one of whom was her own father—who all locked arms. With a sickening feeling, Harlow realized they were trying to create a cushion of sorts, just in case she or Ethan fell.

Just keep climbing, she told herself.

"Audrey—hang on, we're coming!" Ethan yelled, but Audrey continued to scream.

Once she was close to the cart, Harlow balanced herself on the ladder and reached up and grabbed one of the Ferris wheel's neon spokes. It was warm in her hands.

"What are you doing?" Ethan shouted as she climbed further up.

"I'm going in!" Carefully, like a gymnast, Harlow swung herself out and dropped lightly into the cart—jostling it slightly—right in front of Audrey and Grace. "Ta-da!" she said raising her hands high. "It's a bird, it's a plane, it's—Super Harlow!"

Audrey was so shocked she stopped flailing and went still.

"Everyone all right in there?" Ethan called from below. "Audrey, are you okay?"

"She's fine," Harlow said. Both Grace and Audrey were quiet and breathing heavily, seemingly too shocked to speak, but they both looked okay. "Aren't you coming in?" she added. Now that Audrey had stopped thrashing around, the cart was easing back into its resting position.

"On second thought, no." Ethan looked up at her. "I'll go back down and tell everyone things are fine up here. . . . By the way," he called as he began descending the ladder. "I like your face better when you're not wearing a mask!"

After his voice faded away, Grace managed to crack a smile. "Super Harlow?" she said.

Harlow shrugged. "I wanted to make a grand entrance. . . . Wow," she added as she looked down at the crowd below. "There are *a ton* of people pointing their phones at us. What do you want to bet someone down there was hoping one of us would fall because it would make a good picture? Audrey—I'll bet you'll get a *ton* more followers tonight." She looked over at Audrey and blushed. "Sorry—I sort of check your online stuff all the time."

"It's okay," Audrey said. She groaned and clutched her stomach. "I don't feel so good."

"Close your eyes and take deep breaths," Harlow advised. Her phone pinged with a text from Julia:

Since Audrey is okay now they're going to see if they can get the ride fixed. You guys might be up there for a while.

Thanks, Harlow texted back.

On the seat next to her was a brown shoebox, which she picked up. Was this the box Julia had talked about? She reached for the lid. Grace yelled, "Don't open it!" and ripped the box from Harlow's hands.

"It's a prank," Grace said. "From Julia and Erin. That's why I wrote the pumpkin gram."

"Wait—*you* wrote it?" Harlow said. "I'm confused."

"Yeah . . . I think we have a lot to talk about," Grace said.

"Can we do it later?" Audrey asked, breathing deeply. "When we're *not* stuck up here?"

Harlow nodded and said, "Do you want to hold my hand?"

"Yeah," Audrey said shakily. "I really do."

They grasped hands and Harlow stared at the shoe-box. "I'm pretty sure I saw Erin carrying this on the way to the carnival. What do you think is inside?"

"Knowing Julia and Erin, something nasty," Grace said. She turned to Harlow. "They've gotten really mean this last year."

Harlow paused, not sure how to respond. She wanted to say things weren't so simple. That more and more she was beginning to believe everyone wore a mask of sorts. An invisible one, true, but just as real as the one she'd worn earlier that evening. And that she'd gotten a glimpse behind Julia's mask tonight—behind the pranks and the meanness and the shiny Internet images—to the person underneath, a girl who dreamed of arriving to the theater in a pink party dress and wished she could live in a big house like Harlow's. A girl who was willing to spend the last hours of the carnival helping Harlow with her project.

But since she didn't really know how to say all that, Harlow settled for saying, "What could possibly be so bad in there? Dare me to open it?"

Before anyone could say anything, with her free hand she reached out, lifted the lid, and peered inside—then froze.

"You look like you've seen a ghost," Grace said. "What is it? What's inside?"

Harlow just shook her head, unable to speak. It was the one thing she was afraid of; the only dare she'd ever turned down.

"Spi-spi-spiders," she sputtered. She didn't know how Julia and Erin had managed it, but inside were spiders, hundreds of them. Her heart was beating wildly and her fingers were curled like claws around the lid. She couldn't move. She could barely breathe. As she watched, a spider crawled out of the box and began inching toward her thumb. *Help!* she tried to say, but her muscles had seized up and she couldn't open her mouth.

Grace ripped the box out of Harlow's reach and tossed it over the side of the cart. The three of them watched as it spun, end over end as it fell, landing with an audible *thwack*—right on top of Julia's upturned face. Julia began to dance around and brush furiously at her hair.

"Oops," Grace deadpanned. "Looks like Julia just got a spider shower."

At that, Audrey finally snapped out of her daze and began laughing. Harlow and Grace joined in, and Harlow thought being stranded in the sky with the two best friends she'd ever had wasn't a bad way to end the strangest night of her life.

▶ 38 ◀

Grace

FORTY MINUTES LATER, AMID MUCH cheering, the Ferris wheel finally started moving again. A crowd surrounded Grace, Audrey, and Harlow as soon as they stepped off the ride. Mrs. Chang pulled Grace into a suffocating bear hug and began to cry.

Grace hated crowds. And hugs.

But what she hated the absolute most was fighting with her mother, so she made herself hug her back and say, "I'm okay, Mom. I promise."

"Really?" Mrs. Chang pulled away and stared hard at her daughter, as if to make sure.

Grace glanced away from her mother's scrutiny. She saw Mr. McKinley and Ethan talking to Audrey, and Harlow was enveloped in a hug from both her parents. Diego and Mr. Martinez were standing some feet away, chatting with the firemen, who were just about to leave. Mrs. King was combing spiders out of Julia's hair, while Mr. King was saying, "You better hope none of them laid any eggs in there." Julia caught Grace's gaze and shrugged sheepishly; Grace couldn't help but grin back a little.

Mrs. Chang, who finally seemed convinced Grace was all right, sighed and said, "So . . . you decided to go to the carnival even though you're grounded?" She phrased it as a question, and Grace knew there were several wrong answers she could give.

She also knew the best defense is a good offense. Plus, she was still mad.

"So what? You *lied* to me. You said you've been going to your book club on Friday nights—but you've been dating Mr. Martinez!"

"I didn't—" Mrs. Chang stopped. "I wasn't intentionally trying to lie to you. I just wanted to see if things were going anywhere before I bothered you about it."

"And?" Grace said. "Are things going anywhere?"

Mrs. Chang shook her head. "Turns out we both just miss your dad. We spent most of our time talking about him."

Grace really wanted to believe her mother. "Diego said his dad was planning to visit you in California."

"His old college roommate lives in California. He visits there every few years. So yes, on his next trip he said he would come see us if he could squeeze it in. I promise you, we're just friends. It was nice being able to talk to someone about your dad. I miss him."

"*I* miss him too—and I don't want to leave Clarkville," Grace blurted. "I just . . . I don't want to forget." She didn't say anything more, but she knew her mother would understand.

"Oh, Grace—you won't forget him," Mrs. Chang said softly. "Neither of us will. Memories are like pieces of luggage you can't lose because you carry them in your

heart. We're not leaving him. We're taking him with us."
She sighed. "We're renting our house here, not selling it.
You know why I did that? So we could come back some-
day if we want to. I just need to get away for a while.
And Chrissy says I'll always have a place in her salon. So
I'd like you to keep an open mind. Besides, where we're
moving is near the ocean. You could even walk there—I
think you'll like it."

Actually, Grace was pretty sure she'd hate it. She
didn't like sand. Or being wet.

But the thought that they could one day come back
to Clarkville made her feel a little better. And besides,
she and her mother would have several hours in the car
over the next couple days to talk.

"I know I'm grounded and all, but . . . could I go
over to Harlow's house tonight?" As Grace expected,
her mother seemed to swell with indignation.

"You're really asking me that?" Mrs. Chang said.
"You sneak out of the house and—"

"It's for something Harlow is doing," Grace put in
quickly. "Something to help get the factory rebuilt."

Quickly Grace filled her in on the project. "Harlow told me all about it while we were stuck up there waiting for the ride to get fixed. She says she's staying up all night if that's what it takes to get it finished. Audrey says she'll come over too, if her dad will let her, and . . . please, mom? It's my last night in Clarkville. I want to end it with them."

Her mom's anger seemed to deflate. "Well . . . ," she said, and glanced over uncertainly at Mr. and Mrs. Carlson, who nodded at her. "I guess that's okay." She sighed, and her voice went soft, "I guess maybe that's the way things are supposed to be."

After Grace allowed herself to be hugged one last time, Mrs. Chang turned away to say goodbye to Mr. Martinez. Diego was standing a few feet away from them, smiling at Grace.

"Crazy night, huh?" he said.

"Yeah." Grace plunged her hands into her pockets, feeling suddenly shy. She hadn't forgotten that right before she made her mad dash to the Ferris wheel the two of them had been on their way to the Kissing Booth.

Diego seemed to be thinking along the same lines, because he said, "We could still go. To the Kissing Booth, I mean."

Grace glanced at her mother. Could she and Diego get away with visiting one more attraction before they all left the carnival? When she turned back, she saw Diego checking his reflection on his phone.

"What are you doing?" she asked.

"Getting ready to take our selfie," he answered. With his free hand he picked a stray popcorn kernel from his teeth.

"A selfie?" Grace repeated.

"Yeah. Isn't that the whole point of the Kissing Booth—to get a good selfie?"

Grace hadn't known until that exact moment that it was possible to love someone for years from afar—and then fall out of love with them in the space of a single second once you got up close. She felt the weight of it squeezing her heart, but then she remembered:

Diego didn't like carousels. Or baseball.

Who doesn't like baseball?

"Actually," Grace said, "I think I have to leave pretty soon. Why don't you ask someone else to take a selfie with you?" She pointed to Julia, who was still picking spiders from her scalp.

Grace turned away, wondering just how differently this whole night might have gone if only she hadn't destroyed Julia's pumpkin gram to Diego.

She was so lost in thought that she nearly smacked into Mr. McKinley, who'd been passing by. He jerked back so quickly he nearly toppled over. "Grace, I'm so sorry," he said. "I wasn't watching where I was going."

Grace stared into his sad eyes. For the first time in a year she didn't see the person her dad had died trying to save. She saw one of his best friends; someone who had loved him, maybe even as much as she herself had loved him.

And suddenly, she knew why the carousel had granted one of her wishes tonight. She reached into her pocket and pulled out her dad's ring. "Here," she said, pushing it into his hands. "He would have wanted you to have it."

Mr. McKinley was as still as a statue as he stared at the ring. Then he dropped to the ground and his shoulders began to shake.

And even though Grace hated hugs, she put her arm around his shoulders and whispered, "He loved you, Mr. McKinley. I know he did."

▶ EPILOGUE ◀

Six Months Later

NOT EVERY WISH YOU MAKE COMES TRUE, but if you're lucky, sometimes the most important ones do. Sometimes all it takes is a small, unexpected gesture. A hug, freely given from someone who hates them, to someone who's been hating himself.

It's amazing, really, how powerful that gesture can be.

It can break the ice; it can cause tears to flow. It can begin to mend broken hearts.

The girl who does not like hugs arrived in California as a girl who speaks her thoughts. As it turns out, Grace does not hate California. Or the ocean. In fact, she sort of loves them both. It's April, but sunny and warm as she makes her way to her favorite spot by the shore. The port of Long Beach curves to her right. To the left, if she strains her eyes across the sparkling blue sea, she can just glimpse the outline of Catalina Island.

Grace listens to the surf pounding the shore and runs her finger over her dad's old ring. Mr. McKinley, when he could finally find his voice, had pushed it back into her hands and said, "I can't take it. He would have wanted you to keep it." Grace wears it every day on a chain around her neck, close to her heart.

Grace watches as the tide rolls in. The wind has picked up; soon it will be time to go home. Her phone buzzes in her pocket. Harlow has sent her a text:

Five minutes to curtain!

Along with the text there's a picture of Audrey and Mrs. McKinley. They're both smiling, and Audrey is dressed up as Juliet Capulet.

Audrey didn't get a part in *Middle School Daze*, but she *did* get the lead in the school play. Most important, she got her mother back. Things are not perfect at the McKinley household, but they are much better.

Tell Audrey I said break a leg, Grace texts back.

I will. See you soon!

Tomorrow, Grace and her mother are getting on a plane and flying back to Clarkville. The day after that, the Carlsons are breaking ground on the new factory. Grace and her mother are their honored guests.

Well, it won't *actually* be a factory. It'll be a call center. Times are changing, and Mr. Carlson decided he would change too. He's named it the Henry Chang Call Center. The money came in after all, thanks in large part to the presentation Harlow put together. Harlow has no shortage of people wanting to be her friend now, but most days she and Audrey prefer spending time together by themselves. Ethan often joins them, and Audrey has secretly prepared herself for the day her best friend and her twin brother finally decide to become a couple.

Grace has made a lot of new friends in California, even though she still wears her lucky Cubs cap nearly every day. She likes to tell them about the night she got her two best friends back. About the wishes she made on the carousel and her midnight ride on the Ferris wheel. It's one of her favorite things to do. Because when it comes to the Carnival of Wishes and Dreams, everyone has a story to tell.

Grace's phone buzzes with another text from Harlow: My dad and I will pick you guys up from the airport. He says to send him your flight info.

Okay, Grace texts back. See you tomorrow!

Grace puts her phone away and stares at the waves. She loves the ocean, but she can't wait to return to Clarkville.

After all, the people she loves live there.

Acknowledgments

When I was younger, one of the highlights of the year for me was attending the fall festival at St. Bonaventure Catholic Parish in Huntington Beach. The lights, the music, the rides, and the giddiness of an autumn Friday night made an impression on me, and I always knew I'd one day write a book about a carnival.

This book wouldn't exist without the love and support of so many who came alongside me while I was writing it: Kerry Sparks, agent extraordinaire; Alyson Heller and the whole team at Simon & Schuster, who love me and my book babies well; Cara Lane, who told me stories about the carnival in her hometown of Morton, Illinois; and Carrie Diggs and Suzette Leger, who call me up and invite me to lunch and remind me that getting out of my writing cave and socializing is a Good Thing.

To Stefanie Wass, my critique partner: thank you for putting up with my crazy first drafts! My books are always better because of your input!

To the Journey Girls—Ann Davis, Carrie Diggs,

Ruth Gallo, Cara Lane, and Sarah Mahieu: there is magic when the six of us are together. I am so grateful for each one of you.

To my friends and family, who are the best cheering section a girl could ever ask for: thank you. Thanks especially to my grandparents, may they rest in peace, who told me stories about living in the Midwest before moving to California. I thought of you often while I wrote.

To Team NorCal—Adrienne Young, Kristin Dwyer, Stephanie Garber, Joanna Rowland, Jessica Taylor, Shannon Dittemore, and Rose Cooper (We miss you, Rose!): I am so grateful for you guys. You help me keep a sense of humor and perspective when it comes to the writing life.

To Ryan, as we approach our nineteenth wedding anniversary. If I could ride a magic carousel and wish for just one thing, it would be this: to spend another nineteen years living this crazy, wondrous life with you. And thanks be to God; when I was Grace's age, one of my wishes and dreams was to become a published author. Thank you for guiding me on this path.

About the Author

Jenny Lundquist is the author of multiple middle-grade and young adult titles, including *Seeing Cinderella*, *The Charming Life of Izzy Malone*, and *The Wondrous World of Violet Barnaby*. She lives in California with her family and her rescue schnoodle, Ollie the Wonderdog. Visit her online at www.jennylundquist.com or on Instagram @jenny_lundquist.

Looking for another great book?
Find it
IN THE MIDDLE.

Fun, fantastic books for kids
in the in-be**TWEEN** age.

IntheMiddleBooks.com

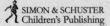